E. A. BAGBY

Illyia

The Feigned Moon of Entiria Epic Serial, Episode Two

Recap

Each episode of this serial picks up where the last left off. Below is a recap of the first episode: The Journey.

Background

Giels Deo, 18, the son of his tribe's Lead Storyteller (mother) and Lead Shaman (father), is heir to a bloodline from the founding members of the Deo Tribe, which is named after their family. The tribe resides in the Deo forest, within the mortal realm—the world between the earth and sky.

Before the story begins, Giels spends months studying oral tradition to become the tribe's next Lead Storyteller.

Most people spend their lives socializing and sustaining themselves by gardening, hunting, and creating tools and other necessities with the help of specialized computers inhabited by the computer spirit. Few honored tribal roles, such as Lead Storyteller, with their accompanying benefits, are available, making it an attractive option for Giels.

Recap

Giels leaves his studies and finds Cleo, his assumed betrothed. But to Giels's chagrin, he learns she's been spending much of her time with their mutual friend Erikal while Giels has been working hard.

Overwhelmed by seeing Cleo after months of being apart,

Giels leans in to kiss her for the first time. But Erikal shows up, interrupting and surprising Giels by gifting him a never-before-seen item of a legend he'd designed on his computer: a voice recorder. Erikal also invites Giels to join him, Cleo, and their friends Meritus and Alana on an adventure in his new floating vehicle.

But going on the journey would mean Giels would miss demonstrating his skills before the Council of Seven Elders, risking his Lead Storyteller role. This puts Giels in a quandary: prove his talents to the tribe or allow Erikal more time alone with Cleo—this time in romantic, distant lands.

Cleo learns that Giels's recorder has a cryptic message asking that the device be brought to some unknown location. She believes Erikal has figured out where and plans to go there on his adventure. Despite believing the recorder's message is a prank by Erikal and Meritus, Giels refuses to be left behind while Cleo goes off. He caves to her pressure to join them.

At the journey's onset, Giels learns that his friends believe the message is a directive to return a ghost within the recorder to the sacred Wind Cave, where lost souls exit the mortal world. Giels, more familiar with lore than his friends, knows that gods and spirits would not do this. So, he demands they turn around immediately, allowing him to prove his storytelling prowess to the council at the rehearsal.

But it's too late. They cannot return up the steep gorges and its massive waterfalls in the storm that rages.

Giels begins to accept that joining his friends will ruin his chance at the important tribal Lead Storyteller role. The weather improves, however, giving him renewed hope, but it's just as they arrive at the sacred cave.

The wind coming from the cave is too strong to toss Giels's

recorder into it as a way to do Salihandron's bidding, as his friends suggested. So, to Giels's relief, they prepare to return home.

He still has a chance to return in time to save his future if they're fast.

But it's not to be. Erikal decides to test his miraculous vehicle by flying into the sacred cavern, despite it being the passage to the Underworld, the land of the dead, and supposedly impossible to enter.

They push through the wind to Giels's terror, ending up in a giant metal tunnel that seems to draw Erikal's vehicle ever deeper.

Shocked by the realm not matching what Giels imagined from the ancient stories, he implores Erikal to go back. But when they find a door out of the tunnel, Giels discovers his bravery and encourages his friends to explore.

Opening the door, they find vast open space defined only by mechwork: pipes, latticework, and machinery—like the bowels of a great machine.

Giels realizes the Underworld doesn't match their mythology. Yet, he believes they'd found the Maze of Azer, where, according to lore, a devil—the Guardian—dwells. The beast's only purpose is to prevent mortals from entering the land of the dead. At worst, it will destroy a person's soul. At best, it will turn a person mad.

It is then that the great, threatening winged beast appears. It attacks, but an alien flying craft fires at the creature, and the devil retreats. As Giels flees, a godlike voice in his head tells him he's needed in the Underworld. It feels like insanity.

He and his friends escape to the world between the earth and sky and race home.

Terrified the Guardian cursed him with madness, Giels grows angry at Erikal for bringing them into the cave. But Cleo seems invigorated.

Clamoring for normalcy, Giels returns home in the dark of night and immediately resumes his studies, despite missing the rehearsal and messing up his future as the Lead Storyteller.

Epilogue

The main story is followed by a short chapter titled "Other Voices," which is repeated in full here:

Far, very far, below the Maze of Azer, in an empty, desolate place, a young, immortal woman sat cross-legged. She listened to the thoughts of an ancient one who occupied a space much farther below than she. The contents of the man's mind flew to her faster than time.

"You cannot allow him to stay home. But understand that he will soon become important to his tribe, making your job more difficult."

Other Voices II

The immortal girl stood and talked to the air. "How did the enemy draw the boy out of his world? Have they used Terminal?"

"We cannot yet say." The ancient one's thoughts traversed vast distances and stretched through her, like a thin wind inside her body. "But the dogmatist, whom you call the enemy, evidently recognizes the boy's importance."

She no longer needed a translator, though she still struggled with his superior language. It communicated in many layers that rose to her mind as a rich, silvered voice. Its deeper tiers had always eluded her, but now, she understood one for the first time: The enemy looked for the boy because they partially understood Terminal.

"Have you discovered anything of their tactic?" she asked.

"They penetrated the balanced world with an idea—a message in the electromagnetic spectrum. They found our artifice and sent a lure."

She lay down on the massive structural beam under her feet. It was one in a multitude of endless arrays of tapered, white girders. In every direction, the arrays twisted like swirling logarithmic spirals into hazy, white vanishing points. She looked for answers in the patterns—answers in her ever-expanding consciousness.

The enemy's intrusion into the boy's realm was what they had hoped for, yet she wrinkled her brow with fear. "Balance was our ancient promise. Every time something enters the domain, we put everything at risk."

"This was not our intrusion." The response sounded more like lead than silver. She detected no subtleties in it, no hidden layers.

"It was our intrusion," she said. "We placed what you call an artifice. Call him what he is—bait! Oh, I still do not understand the immortal mind. You want me to lead innocence to the maw."

"If the boy does not leave, the dogmatist will need to physically enter his world."

With Terminal, the enemy might someday do the unthinkable. They might not only learn how to enter the boy's world, but also, eventually, they may enter hers.

Tears rolled off of her cheeks onto the beam. Her chest ached. She swallowed and turned her head to the side in anticipation of the sensations to follow.

Her toes and fingers seared. The heat went up her arms, spreading until her body and psyche raged. The pain, loud and pure, rose in a chorus like the screams of a thousand primal souls. Her pupils rolled up past open eyelids.

This will end . . . someday soon my feelings will diminish.

The raging storm calmed enough for her to speak. "You predict that the boy may not leave again because he'll be too important."

"His fate depends on ceremony."

"Then I'll open the sky with rain and lightning until they see an omen. You tell me when, and I'll ruin him!"

1

Only One Day

Above me, the god Etargoren's lightning fizzled across the roiling grey sky.

To hide my recorder's blue light, I dropped it into a pocket. I kneeled in the tall swamp-grass and breathed only during the soft crackling of the god's electric display.

The lightning did not boom, which would have scared the game; it was gentle and stayed in the sky. Nor did Tohillocen cry her rain.

Rustling in the bushes beyond the small clearing caught my attention. With my aluminum spear balanced between my thumb and forefinger, I lifted my arm little by little like the movement of a branch in the breeze. But the rustling stopped.

I exhaled, relieved. In truth, I wanted an excuse to remain here, far from people.

Ten days had passed since Erikal had given me the recorder, three days since we left on our journey. Less than a day ago, the soul-destroying Guardian of the deep gazed upon me with pupilless eyes.

Only one day. I hadn't recovered.

After Erikal had dropped me off, I sat in the dark on my bed, practicing my Equis recitation. I needed that normalcy. And I needed, for the moment, to believe the shamans would still consider me for the role of Lead Storyteller, as though I hadn't broken their rule by skipping the rehearsal.

I needed my life unchanged.

A couple of hours after my return, I quickly showered, dressed, and took the long walk to the Rambles by the light of the unusually bright moons. My parents hadn't had a chance to confront me.

The Sun had since risen. All around, light grey remains of dead trees poked high above tangled bushes, dark water, and grasses. The few living trees grew crooked and short, half of their branches broken and pallid. I waited at the edge of a rare dry spot where game liked to sniff out slugs and insects.

It was all silent and still, except for the lightning god above.

A cry, like a girl's wailing, rang out in the quiet landscape— probably some unknown lizard. The smell of decay floated on the breeze. Years ago, Elder Sparus had claimed that a rotting, half-dead girl wandered the trails here, drowning the living. Chills ran down my arms, even though I had never believed him.

Few others visited the Rambles, so it had always been a place for me to think and clear my head.

But this time, thinking might have been risky. My entire body screamed with disappointment and rage.

I had gone on the adventure and endangered my future for Cleo. All of her talk about Erikal made me fear losing her. But the two had not flirted at all, and she had held my hand in the otherworldly Maze of Azer, making me realize that little had changed between us. I had done something uncharacteristic, panicked, and made a rash judgment.

Or did I go for reasons other than Cleo?

Like the animals sneaking in the swampy murk, something stirred under my surface thoughts. But what? I hadn't gone from some notion of being in my own adventure, my own story, like the heroes of old. After I had suggested this idea to Cleo, it trickled like a stream somewhere in my mind. But the stream slowly died. Maybe my motivation was just to make a decision while everyone—my parents, Erikal, Cleo—pushed me in conflicting directions.

Only, Erikal brought me somewhere forbidden against my will.

Damn. My fingers tightened around the spear shaft. The dank marshland flickered with the lightning. Even if the council would forgive me for being gone, I'd probably have to work doubly hard to become what I was meant to—the Lead Storyteller.

A creature scurried in the bushes beyond the clearing. Its little, whiskered nose popped out from the tangled leaves.

The ramble-rodent skipped into the open while I rose in the shade of a scrubby tree. It searched among the grasses for insects, sniffing about with jerking starts and stops. I lifted the weapon, my hand tightening more.

The spear flew forward through the animal's neck, pinning it to the ground. Like most game, it twitched as if in denial of its doom.

How fascinating. The little soul would travel to the Underworld, where I'd been just the day before. That was a strange thought—like gossamer pulled away to reveal a vivid truth my eyes would rather not see. My head became light.

We went through the passage like the dead. The Guardian of the deep gazed upon me.

Despite knowing where we'd gone, the idea came crashing in

like a sudden realization, ambushing me. It was as visceral as if the electric storm above had erupted in my head. I put a hand to my temple to steady my mind while the world in my eyes rolled sideways.

Another assault came from within, this one a phrase from ancient lore.

"*. . . all in the world between the earth and sky must die.*"

I stumbled to the spear, still lodged in the animal and the earth, and grabbed it to support myself. A memory came unbidden like a vivid dream.

* * *

Cleo and I sat on the flagstone floor of my home's courtyard. We held figurines of cotton, sticks, and cloth. Toys. We were six or seven.

"I know what we can do," Cleo said. "Tell the story your mother did."

"What story?"

She lowered her voice to an ominous whisper, and her eyes grew large. "The Underworld one."

"*The Journey of Salihandron?* Okay, but I'll start where the Original People escaped."

I held out my shaman figurine and recited, "Salihandron grew furious and blew hard into the cave to keep human souls where they belonged—in the Underworld, subjugated to the gods of the deep."

Cleo wrapped her arms tight around one of mine. "What's 'subjectated'?"

"*Subjugated.* It's sort of—" I thought about what it meant. "Those gods were mean to people, made them do all of their work."

"That's terrible. *Subjugated.* I'll remember that." Her arms squeezed tighter. "You know so much. You can tell me stories every day, forever."

I agreed and continued:

> *But the Sun and Dayodec, the earth-mother, seeing the Original People's determination, wanted them in the world between the earth and sky.*
>
> *Salihandron relented and reversed its breath's direction, blowing the people out from the Underworld into the mortal world beyond the exit.*
>
> *Mortals are in balance with the heavens and the Underworld. So, Salihandron forever blows its wind through the exit to keep the living out, protecting the mortal world from the knowledge of the deep. This exit is what we know as the Wind Cave.*
>
> *Salihandron agreed to escort the souls of the dead back to their home in the Underworld. There, they wandered the darkness, as they do today, until their stars fell from the heavens, blinding the souls' memories of past lives and the spirit realm.*
>
> *The Original People did not protest, because they did not yet know mortal life.*
>
> *But, soon, the Original People understood the cycle of life and forgetting, and that all in the world between the earth and sky must die.*

The shaman toy was me, and I, him. I imagined myself a respected elder, like my father. I shook the cloth-covered figure as he told the story.

"That's all I memorized," I said. "My mother recited it to me only a couple times. It doesn't rhyme, either."

Cleo smiled, shivering with excitement. "It's really creepy. Make up the rest."

"Good idea," I said, holding out my toy. "I'm a great shaman, and I say, 'I'll get you, Salihandron Soul-Herder!'—"

My mother walked into the courtyard with her mouth stretched in a toothy smile; she still had her youthful beauty. I had thought she would always be young, inspiring me to smile back at her in a child's delight of it all.

She leaned down. "Giels, we have very good news for you. Your father and I have been talking quite a lot about this." Her eyes brightened. "You will be able to take after me and be a Storyteller. And, you may be one of the greatest ever in the Deo."

The toys in my hand died, killed by the Salihandron of my imagination and my mother's words. I left Cleo in the courtyard and wrapped myself in my bed covers. The regal little cloth man was lost to the dust under my bed, never again to be a shaman.

* * *

Lightning crackled above, catching my eye. I shuddered, startled to be in the Rambles. Layers of time had buried that moment somewhere in the dark reaches of my mind.

Cleo's sweet words made me smile for a second.

I had forgotten I wanted to be a shaman. Most young boys and girls romanticized the idea at one point.

Lead Storytellers and shamans both ran in my family. I scoffed. Becoming an elder of the council would have required training throughout childhood and adolescence, much harder than becoming a storyteller, even the Lead Storyteller. After a life of grueling training, they ended up being pestered with other people's problems. Sure, people revered elders and followed their wisdom, but not having the magic to actually be one was fortunate.

The memory reinforced what I knew and what I would have to remind the council of: my ability to memorize words, and that storytelling could not have been more ideal. Lore that took other storytellers years to learn, I perfected in a few months.

Except the ancient stories do not describe the Underworld that I saw.

I closed my eyes and took a deep breath to push the journey out of my mind. The place seemed too unfathomable.

I slid the ramble-rodent carcass off of the spear, gutted the arm-length creature with my laser, and wrapped it in cloth. I meant to thank it for becoming food, but "sorry" escaped my lips instead.

Something rustled nearby. Spear already in hand, I twisted my torso and let it fly. Another ramble-rodent, this one larger. Two kills in one day was an admirable feat for such a rare creature. I put aside the idea they were part of a family.

I had gone hunting to avoid seeing my parents. I wasn't ready for their disappointment, nor did I want their faces to reflect my own.

The moment would need to come.

Perhaps two fatty ramble-rodents would soften their reprimands.

Besides, Elder Sparus's undead girl or no, I feared the landscape's spirits had been rising from the dark water to infect me.

Slipping out of the stagnant marsh, I washed up at a clear

puddle and walked along the trail leading east to my home in the Old Neighborhood. At the main north-south intersecting path, I stopped and faced south, towards the sparse and austere South Neighborhood and Cleo's home.

Cleo had told me I would be the Lead Storyteller, whether or not I missed the rehearsal, as though my father and the council would make sure I somehow gained the role. Now I wondered if she had just wanted to prod me because of my hesitation about going with her.

She also suggested we could kiss after our adventure. I took a step to the south.

"Giels!" a familiar voice called from behind.

I spun around. A cab floated just behind me on the way leading north. For a quick second, I thought it was the Silver Dare. But with its smaller size and more straightforward jointing and wing design, it was Meritus's facsimile of Erikal's vehicle.

The door was up, and Meritus stuck his head out sideways.

"Don't sneak up on me like that," I said.

He laughed, but I didn't. Usual Meritus, light and peppy, as if we hadn't just witnessed the soul-sucking demon.

"Are you bringing those to our gathering?" he asked.

"What?"

"Don't be modest. I see what you have there."

I glanced at the creatures draped over my forearm.

"The others will be there around five or six," he added.

"Gathering?"

"Ah, Alana was supposed to tell you. But apparently you were hunting. It's about you-know-what. What we should do now, or something. Erikal's idea. I just need to drop off some items first, and I'll go over." He waved me out of the way and moved the vehicle up beside me. "Personally, I can't wait to tell everyone about the monster. And that wingless vehicle. Is your head not just going crazy!" His eyes widened and his smile stretched, revealing all of his teeth, like pure, honed alabaster in the stubble of his thin face. He pulled the door down and headed south, probably towards Erikal's home.

Tell everyone? How did I not think to warn him? A cold chill shot down my sides. *Oh, hell, Meritus.*

Before us, none had dared to enter the cave. The repercussions of doing so could be brutal.

The council cannot find out.

If entering the Wind Cave was the utmost taboo, misleading the shamans was an easy second. "Don't deceive the council" was a common phrase. And for good reason. Public shaming, banishment, separating people who conspire from ever seeing each other, and exclusion from tribal events had all been consequences of lying, sometimes lasting a lifetime.

But silence is not deception if the council doesn't ask questions. Is it?

"Meritus! Don't say anything!" I shouted. His cab turned out of view. "Dammit."

Throwing the two weighty kills and the spear under my arm, I sprinted on the winding trail after him, kicking up dust. At a long, straight run of the path, his vehicle should have been in view. It had disappeared.

Given he'd been rash enough to go into the Wind Cave, would Erikal have considered the repercussions? Would Cleo and Alana? I needed to find them. Meritus would go along with what Erikal wanted if he could keep his mouth shut in the meantime.

A hazy Sun glowed through the canopy of enormous oaken trees. Based on the blue orb's position, the afternoon edged towards four, if not later. The others might have already been at our gathering spot.

I had little time. Ever since Meritus had started his nightly cab races months ago, scores of youths gathered at our spot when the sky yellowed at dusk. I couldn't risk my friends saying something to them.

My parents' scoldings would need to wait.

Turning on my heel, I raced to the commons.

2

Among the Moss

For forty-five minutes, I ran.

The entire way to the commons, it seeped into my mind how strongly the council might react to us entering the cave. Traditional lore made going in seem impossible, so I hadn't ever thought about the repercussions. Still, many stories described the act as the most heinous offense.

The living belonged in the mortal world.

While the shamans had doled out severe punishments for being lied to, my father once described their most somber ostracism, one they hadn't ever had to use: the council praying for damnation—for no possibility of rebirth after death. Harsh. But if that punishment was meant for anything, leaving the World would be it.

My friends and I needed to coordinate.

After spotting a hodgepodge of youths at our usual meeting place, I stopped so abruptly that I tumbled to the moss. The side of my head pressed on the green carpet, and the ramble-rodents and spear lay scattered.

Through the forest of widely dispersed Deo trees, several

people lounged, ones I knew a little or not at all.

None of the adventurers had arrived.

The Sun brightened the overcast sky in the west. A crowd didn't normally gather until the Sun sat on the horizon, another hour or two away.

Why were they there? What had Meritus told them? The dread that had already engulfed me grew intolerable. If Meritus had said something, I would lie. The council frowned upon dishonesty, but I'd never heard of youths getting in trouble for lying to one another.

I'll say Meritus tricked them.

I stood, grabbed the rodents, and took a moment to catch my breath and straighten my clothes. Then I approached casually, with my hand in a pocket.

The lightning had stopped. The thick, grey sky cast the commons in a muted glow. Despite the dimmer light, the perfectly flat, moss-covered ground, thick tree trunks, and canopy of broad leaves stood out with vivid color under the clouds. Few animals called at that time of day, adding to the calm and making it feel like an indoor living area. It had an intimate mood perfect for divulging our unthinkable journey.

Fairfox, a friend of Cleo's, shouted in her bright, high-pitched voice as I drew close, "Perfect, you brought food!" She sat cross-legged, her tiny frame straight and her head high. On a finger twirled a copper datch, a flying discus with a handle on its underside. This one had fancy geometric etchings of intertwined circles.

Fairfox flicked her wrist, and the disc shot my way. "What do you think? Just made it."

I caught the datch with my free hand and, making a full rotation with my arm, tossed it back. "Smooth."

Except for them being early, so far, everything seemed ordinary.

Fairfox placed the disc in her lap. "Something happened, didn't it?"

My legs nearly buckled under me, but I maintained my casual gait.

"He's being quiet about it," she said. "Suspicious."

The scent of charring spar, a root vegetable, filled the air. Someone had set up a flame grill a short distance from where the group sat.

"Nothing happened," I said, and headed in the direction of the grill with a bounce in my step. "Nothing I know of." I could pretend that nothing was out of the ordinary and Meritus was lying, but at some point, he and the others would show up. The five of us would need to have a serious discussion without this group knowing.

A girl I remembered by her long, thin face, more handsome than pretty, stood. Her name came to me—Serina. "She means something happened with Cleo, Erikal, and Meritus, and . . ." She talked with the forceful tone of the North Neighborhood, where people tended to be brash and exaggerate their *r*'s. "What's that other girl's name, the one that usually leaves when everyone else shows up? Elna?"

"Alana."

Serina squinted her striking light-brown eyes. "I think they haven't been around because of"—she threw her arm out and pointed at me—"you."

Me? I barely knew Serina. What did she know about me?

"With you busy," she added, smiling, "why come so far to be with us rabble? Definitely found a new spot closer to their homes."

I winced all of the way to the flame-grill. "Why are all of you here? It's early." They probably thought me standoffish, which was fine. Maybe they would realize they were imposing.

"Is that a problem?" Fairfox said. "If being here's a problem, blame Meritus."

Panic shot up my spine. I turned to the grill away from them to hide my shock. "What did he say?" I hoped to sound disinterested.

"Nothing. Just that everyone would be here. Why? Didn't he tell you?"

That's all he said?

"Cleo and Erikal haven't been here for a while," Fairfox said. "He probably figures he can start racing early. I played datch with Serina and told her, and she told Zara and Samsen, who—"

"That's great," I said, cutting her off. I liked Fairfox, but at that moment, I had no patience for her chirpy mood.

I dropped my ramble-rodents on the grill's side counter, glad to be free of the heavy load.

They didn't know. Not yet. Now I just needed to make sure they didn't find out.

Perhaps cooking would calm my nerves. After hiding a rodent in a side drawer, I grabbed a prepping knife and slid it under the furry hind leg of the other.

"They had an argument," Fairfox said with the confidence of someone solving a riddle. "Somebody's upset. By the sound of it, I might know who." Her datch whizzed past me, far into the trees. A boy jumped and caught it. He walked in our direction and tossed it back over my head.

"Hi, Giels," the boy said. Had I met him? I glanced around. More came towards us from every direction; some walked, while others floated in their cabs.

Unbelievable. How did Meritus not understand the situation?

"Maybe they're jealous Giels will have a title," Serina said.

"What?" I shouted. Her commentary was the last thing I needed.

Somebody approached from behind with solid and quick footfalls on the moss. I didn't turn. "We're just concerned," Serina said, the soft sounds of her breath near my ear. I nearly jumped up. "Our nightly gatherings started because of you guys. You have your Equis practicing, but where're the rest?"

Somehow, they had to stop asking questions.

"Giels!" Alana called from a short distance away. "There you are."

I slowly exhaled, and my shoulders dropped. I almost ran and hugged her. Alana was the only other person on our adventure who'd thought it was mad. But I stayed put. I didn't want to give the others more reasons to speculate.

She bustled through the trees looking clean and fresh and, in fact, spunky in her short, white dress.

I felt like an exhausted mess.

Coming to my side, Alana placed a hand on the ramble-rodent and squeezed. "A payadekka," she said, in her East Neighborhood vernacular. "A big one. Nice treat." She picked up the knife to finish skinning it.

"I'm glad you're here," I said, and turned to glance behind me. Serina had rejoined the others, her mop of dark-auburn hair shaking as she talked.

"No one else would help you?" Alana asked in her typical soft-spoken voice. She had a tone a little deeper than other girls, but it had a lovely lilt.

I shook my head. "I didn't ask. I mean, they're wondering where we've been. Have you not met here for a while? Fairfox thinks we're fighting."

Alana winced. "She does? We haven't met here since . . . I guess a week before we left, so they could prepare."

"Ah. That's what they're going on about." It had been almost two weeks. *Maybe we should let them believe we're all fighting.*

"Just talk to me if you like," she said.

"With pleasure."

"How're you?"

I shrugged. "Don't know. You?"

"My night was full of strange dreams, some frightening. In one, I am falling and never stop. Ever. But I'm well, otherwise." She stared into my eyes for a moment. What was she trying to see? I blinked and turned. "You look . . . unwell."

"Thanks, just need sleep." I forced a smile, and she smiled back.

I placed a few cuts of meat on the grill. It looked fatty and delicious. The sizzle and aroma grounded me in the World for the first time since our journey. I took a deep inhale.

Alana seemed like someone who might give my concerns the attention they needed. "You know how taboo the cave is, don't you?" I whispered.

She shot me a side glance, furrowing her brow. "I'd assume it would be."

"We can't tell them anything. Anything. If the council—my father—finds out . . . This is *very* bad." I hesitated, thinking of how to say it, but Alana preempted me.

"I know." Her voice cracked. Of course she knew. There were rumors about the big punishment. "Your father— Are *you* safe?" she whispered.

I shook my head. Even if my father wanted to protect me, the other members could dole out the curse if it meant not seeming biased.

Alana might have had an interest in Meritus, so I showed concern on my face and talked slowly. "I'm worried about Meritus. He may not be aware. It's not something that comes up very often, and you know how he sometimes . . ."

She nodded. I stood a little straighter.

Cabs collected around us, parking on the moss in the spaces between trees. Serina and Fairfox continued speculating, pulling new arrivals into the conversation. It hadn't occurred to me before how childish some of them could be.

"Maybe Alana's parents put a spell on Erikal, Cleo, and Meritus," one of the boys said.

Alana scoffed and said quietly to me, "He doesn't even know my parents. If any of our parents did magic, it would be your father."

Finally, I laughed. "I wouldn't trust him to do magic. He might accidentally charm himself."

She didn't laugh in return. Instead, she dropped her hair in front of her face and cut the meat into strips—such a strange, faraway girl.

A familiar vehicle hovered towards us and descended onto its parking legs. Meritus jumped out, whistling a stilted improvisation.

I sighed with relief. "Here he is." We could intercept him before he talked.

He came over and tossed a handful of root vegetables onto the grill, emphasizing the action with the climax of his song. The flames roared like an accompanying instrument from oil and water falling off of the tubers.

I stared at him to get his attention, but he either didn't notice or pretended not to.

"I'll be making a grill twice the length of this one," he said, nudging himself into Alana. If he had an interest in her, it could only be because he wanted someone completely unlike himself—someone thoughtful.

Meritus put a finger to his ear as though listening to the gathering behind us, seemingly oblivious to my steady gaze on him.

I snapped a finger near his head. "We need to talk."

"One moment." With arms out wide, he sauntered to the group, which had swelled to over thirty boys and girls standing around. "Heyyy."

My heart hammered. "Meritus," I said in a low shout. He ignored me. I slammed the laser cutter down. He seldom did what he was told unless it came from Erikal. But maybe Alana had some sway. "He's going to say something."

"I can get his attention." Alana grabbed a plate of food and darted away, bumping past a girl. "Sorry," she exhaled, and pushed through a few others. But the small crowd had absorbed Meritus.

Erikal stepped out of the Silver Dare and Cleo out of her cab. When had they arrived?

Meritus raised his arms and patted the air. "Everyone, let's sit! We have much, so much, to talk about."

"Hell," I cursed under my breath. A few heads close to me snapped to my direction. Those in my Deo lineage were supposed to exude manners.

The gathering casually organized itself into a large circle on the soft moss carpet, habitual when socializing in the commons.

With no space to sit by Meritus, Alana rounded the group towards Cleo and dropped to her right. Erikal took the spot on Cleo's left.

I dared not shush Meritus, not now.

What can I do? Maybe I should just start shouting.

I remained the only one standing, as if stuck in place. My heart continued to race. Pushing my fingers through my hair, I took the only spot remaining, between Alana and Samsen Moss. He, like me, was the son of a council member, Elder Boan Moss, though Samsen was training to be a shaman.

This group liked Samsen, but shamans-in-training stayed close to the council, like an extension of it. He would certainly report whatever he heard.

Thankfully, within the thick din of conversation, I didn't yet detect any talk of our adventure or absence.

Meritus groaned. "Where's Berian when we need some Drink?" Laughter.

A herd of white tassel-goats moved in our direction. They get testy if they think people are in the way of good moss grazing, which gave me hope that they would upend the gathering. But Fairfox tossed her datch and spooked the herd. I started to pull the recorder from my pocket to distract everyone with it, but then I pushed it back down, deep. The journey was within it, as was the message.

Samsen leaned to look past me. "Where've you been?" he barked at Cleo and Erikal.

"We went somewhere in Erikal's new cab, the Silver Dare," Cleo said, and waved to the vehicle.

Oh, shit.

I leaned forward, blocking Samsen's view of her. "Cleo." I tried communicating discretion with a raised eyebrow.

"The what?" Serina said. Her face contorted with overt mockery. "You gave it a name? Who names a vehicle?"

Meritus pulled out a crit, a type of chromadium bass harp,

from his bag. "You would understand"—he plucked a pretty melody of a song about love lost during winter in the north—"if you had gone with us. It's like nothing you've experienced. We entered—"

"Dammit!" I shouted before I could stop myself. Seemingly half the group gasped. "We entered the spiritual realm," I said, by which I meant something akin to a shaman vision quest. It just came out.

I caught Erikal staring at me. Not knowing what else to do, I stared back. His eyes softened a bit, and I thought I detected the slightest nod.

"Giels," Meritus said through his teeth, "if you let me finish my—"

"The Silver Dare took us on an inward, spiritual journey if you will," Erikal interrupted, "and it gave each of us a lot to think about." He looked around, and we, his travelling companions, including Meritus, nodded. So it was with Erikal.

Erikal must have caught on to the danger. Thank the Sun. Hopefully, my friends would now drop the subject.

"Spiritual? In a cab?" Serina said, her dubious expression growing more exaggerated until her entire face screwed up. "You must've gone somewhere."

Erikal waved his hand dismissively. "We went a couple of places. But the place is not as important as what we felt. Going to faraway exotic lands has that effect."

As if to emphasize the point, Meritus hit his harp with a sharp strum.

"So exciting," Fairfox said. "The Deo must feel completely ordinary now." Several others exclaimed their agreement with her.

You have no idea.

Meritus strummed again.

"Our journey inspired all of us," Erikal said. "I'll be working on making a cab larger than the Dare, and Cleo already invented a way to dye her room—would you believe it—sacred yellow. Isn't that right?" He turned to her.

She did?

Another strum.

"Dye your room?" Fairfox said. "Do you mean the bed?" A few boys snickered.

"Oh, no, you must see it, Fairfox. It's not the textiles," Cleo said, "but even better. I've been up all night. I covered part of my ashlar wall in yellow-dyed craft paste. It's so beautiful, and I plan to cover the rest."

Covered her wall? No one had ever permanently coated a wall's natural material.

"And," Erikal said, as the strumming continued, slowly becoming unbearable to me, "Meritus set up a workshop camp near my home, next to the Rambles, complete with a computer and producer under a tarp. Today, he added a sleeping tent. It's fantastic."

What the Sun was going on with them?

"Yeah," Meritus said, "I'm helping with the second Dare and processing Cleo's craft paste. Anyone here can come by. Help me gather more sacred-yellow-dye snails."

"They're so rare," Fairfox said. "Your producer allowed that many?"

Cleo plucked a piece of meat from the platter and handed the dish to her left. "Erikal's computer helped us figure out a way."

"I can't imagine so much yellow," Fairfox said. "Why do it?"

"We passed the threshold." Erikal's voice took on the ominous, formal tone of a storyteller reciting a dire epic. "And at the threshold was a small room of yellow, and in the room a door, and past the door a wondrous world you would not believe." I rubbed my face. It was like the guy rehearsed his soliloquies for hours. I thought he understood the danger, so why was he going on about this?

"We dared not go further," Erikal continued, "because in that place dwelled the Guardian."

The Guardian? Can he not stop talking?

A deep, bass strum.

Samsen snorted. "The Guardian? Impossible. We shamans-in-training are taught that visions quests are for the council. They don't just happen. Tell me, what magical elixir did you use? What spell? What spirit took you?" He rolled his eyes wide.

"Not a spirit, but Salihandron," Meritus said, smiling confidently as though well versed in lore, even though my friends had completely made that part up.

Samsen scoffed.

"Aren't you reciting *The Sun and Moons* at the Equis?" Serina said, looking at me. "The Guardian's in that, isn't it?"

Finally, a change in topic, sort of. I seized on it. "Yes. It includes the beasts' origins, in fact. It's quite a frightening history that—"

"It's quite a frightening history," Serina said, adjusting her voice and accent to mimic me. Several laughed. "You sound all lofty in your Old Neighborhood way of talking." Again, laughter. She stretched herself back on the moss. "Mmmmm. Wish I were a Deo. Full of talent and esteem." Condescension and sarcasm dripped from her words. "Rumor says your cousin Quickleaf Deo will be added to the council at the Equis—the same day you'll become Lead Storyteller. She's only twenty-two, three years older than me."

My heart sank. I already felt the humiliation of the council's likely rejection of me, but at least the topic had changed. *I'll keep it that way.* "I *may* be next in line for Lead Storyteller."

Serina scoffed. "May? There are two truths about the council and storytellers. There are always a couple of Deos on the council, and when was the last time a Deo wasn't Lead Storyteller?"

Just like Cleo. Did everyone believe the council would just give me the title? I had worked hard. My parents exhaustingly reminded me of how much I needed to work to even have a chance, despite my abilities.

"Show us—tell us a little of the Guardian," Serina said. "Let's hear that Deo talent."

I just wanted this gathering to be over. I shook my head. "The part about Dayodec's origins is the best," I said, to try to shift the topic again.

"Go on, we'd love to hear the Guardian's history," Fairfox said with her high, peppy voice. "It could help us understand your vision." She sounded so sincere and delighted.

The strumming continued, rhythmic, endless.

"Meritus, would you stop it with that thing?" I said.

He shrugged and put the instrument down. "Don't see a problem."

Everyone stared at me in anticipation, the magical yellow of dusk cast on their faces. Before I knew it, a groan escaped me.

"Fine," I said, "you want some history? Know that the Guardian poisons the mind, even in a vision." I would make them think it awful enough to drop the subject, and so they'd understand there was nothing romantic about the beast.

After all, a horrid, dreamlike experience is the same as a nightmare.

I decided to recite the most frightening portions for effect:

Of all the fav'rite tales e'er told, no terror's madness is so bold, as of the Guardian tale of old, the beast in the Wind Cave's hold.

Being such a thing as terror, s'no mere accident or error. You think it dwells in just the cave—in that dark and hard enclave? Despite how it would sometimes seem, it lives in us—the hateful scream.

"Ooh," Fairfox said.

I cleared my throat. "This is the important part."

Prior trespass the ever after, one must pass the Maze of Azer. In the maze, went the brothers three. But Secret Knowledge killed their glee. As bright as gold and black as glass, it enters minds, a deathless ghast. As every fear, intent to hold, it's evil, loathsome, vile, and old. It's devil's heart and dead souls' dread, and angry mobs, spirits bled. It's pain and venom, life's vast woes, within one's thoughts' erratic throes.

I skipped to the Guardian's summary.

The knowledge exudes ethereal poison—hate, disgrace, fear, guilt, and paranoia. Their minds and souls and bodies bent with hurt, the brothers trifold joined into devil's cursed.

And thus you learn the Guardian came to be, to guard the Underworld from mortal thee. To see that terror beast within thine eyes, invites sinful knowledge into thine

mind.
With secrets' torments, thoughts of skies above, it ruins
all who pass with hate and love.

During my short recitation, the yellow hues darkened. The day had become night.

My heart raced. Memories of the massive winged creature and its thorny teeth flashed through my mind. I'd almost forgotten about the demon's curse.

The fear I expected to see on everyone else's faces did not materialize. Instead, their eyes sparkled with wonder in the light of the flame-grill, as though the tale excited them.

"Thank you, Giels," Fairfox said, almost breathless. "So, your vision was all just from the magic of a faraway land?"

"That's about right," Meritus said, playing along with Erikal's narrative. "Magic made us see these things. But we didn't mention the cab of the gods that scared the beast away."

Like a private joke, Erikal and Meritus seemed delighted to describe the real journey like it was an imagined one. It took effort for me to stay relaxed.

Samsen snorted with disgust. "You're obviously making this up."

"Making it up?" Fairfox said. "Would they be so inspired if they made it up? I could only imagine having a yellow room."

My recitation may not have frightened Fairfox. But fortunately, Samsen, the one person who might have talked to the council about our vision quest, didn't even believe we'd had one, let alone had gone into the cave during it.

Without Samsen's support, this group should tire of our imagined journey and never know we'd gone to the literal

Underworld.

We went to the literal Underworld. How unreal, even the thought.

"Giels," Fairfox said, "tell the parts with Salihandron."

I stood. I didn't want to hear about how the journey inspired them. "If you want to see me recite, come to the Equis." I walked over to the flame-grill and grabbed the payadekka that I had hid. "I have a lot of real-world responsibilities."

It was time to confront my parents and hopefully recover my path to Lead Storyteller.

"What's wrong with him?" Samsen said.

"He seems fine," Fairfox said. "He's busy. Let's go see Cleo's room and the camp."

They wasted no time. The entire group scrambled into cabs, and in a procession, the vehicles' Sunfire lights angled away from me through the trees, towards the South Neighborhood.

Only home a day, and my friends had turned bizarre.

Erikal could build larger vehicles, Meritus a camp, and Cleo a yellow room without me.

* * *

The glass door in the entrance passage of my home whooshed up to let me through.

"Giels!" my mother cried out from somewhere.

Upon me entering the main living area, my parents shot up from their sitting pillows.

The three of us stood in silence. They stared, pain chiselled into their faces.

"You look exhausted," my mother said.

My father cleared his throat and lifted his chin. The hurt

receded from his expression. "I asked you not to go with Erikal. It's quite a mess that—"

"Never mind," I interrupted. "I'm sorry. It was a mistake. Here." I slammed the ramble-rodent onto a low table. It was their favorite delicacy, which they probably hadn't had in a year.

If Cleo and Serina were right that the council would choose me as Lead Storyteller no matter what, I didn't want the Deo to have reason to believe it. "My recitation will be perfect."

3

The Equis

After the meeting with my friends, my mother and I spent two intense weeks preparing for my recitation.

The day of the Equis ended the hot season and started the mild one. It sat exactly at the midpoint of the year, and the celebration would begin at noon, the center of the day. The timing of the ceremony was, in a sense, perfectly average, and based on the fanfare, that meant it was also ideal.

My father had said little to me after the journey, seemingly to the point of avoidance. But he intercepted me on my way out. "Giels, I— I hope for the best. You have worked hard. Just, well, stay confident."

"Of course I'll stay confident." He had hardly said a thing for weeks, and now was throwing out meaningless, obvious words to sound wise.

Shaman, indeed. Perhaps Serina and Cleo were right that the council gave my family special consideration when deciding on tribal roles. I didn't want that to happen to me.

None of my friends had come to visit since our gathering, except for Alana and Meritus once a couple of days prior. They told me that all of the adventurers set up tents at Meritus's camp, and asked if I wanted one. Why? To help Meritus and Erikal build the new cab and other machines? It wasn't just them. Serina and Fairfox had tents as well. It baffled me. Why live in a tent?

Our "spiritual" adventure had not waned from their imaginations as I hoped. Cleo, apparently, had also been busy applying yellow paste on Fairfox and Serina's bedroom walls.

I reminded Alana and Meritus of the seriousness of keeping our journey secret. I also reminded them that I would be reciting at the main ceremony in the center of the commons, and to bring Cleo and Erikal.

After the fanfare of the day, Cleo and I could finally spend time together—hopefully, alone. She could tell me all about the yellow walls and tents, and maybe I could find out what possessed her to make them.

Our glass entry door slid up and I stepped outside. Just as all of the Deo would have hoped, the Sun gave us a perfect, warm morning. And no other sky god, neither Tohillocen nor Etargoren, intruded on it.

The gods were on my side.

I walked through our garden and jumped across the stream into the commons. All smelled fresh. Wisps of fog snaked around the tree trunks. The leaves brightened under the gaze of the late-morning Sun.

The Deo trees were not very tall—around thirty to forty feet high. At about twenty feet up, branches radiated outward, extending nearly horizontally for another twenty or so feet to where they turned vertical at their tips.

The trunks rose like slightly imperfect, dark columns, the branches flew out like arrayed beams, and the thick foliage above caught my eye—a gorgeously ornate ceiling. Ribbons of azure sky meandered between the canopies like interwoven skylights, allowing the Sunlight to grace the moss. I jumped over each bright, crooked line.

Halla, wild nature, gave the commons no understory growth, making the place like a vast, beautiful building, one significantly grander than could ever be built by people. And that day, the building served one purpose.

I made my way to a place in the commons where a tree had died several years before, and a sapling had yet to replace it. As I arrived, shaman apprentices finished assembling a large, wooden platform in that open space.

People gathered all around, thousands already sitting on outdoor pillows. A number of people put the finishing touches on the abundant vases of flowers and the streamers extending from tree to tree. Rows of flame grills lined the back of the seating area, for the afternoon tassel-goat feast.

Parked vehicles filled an adjacent section of the wood. Elder Sparus's cab descended on its skis there. His door rose on its top hinges, and he and my parents piled out. The three joined me in taking seats to the left of the stage, among other councilmembers, storytellers, and performers.

My mother persistently fussed that I had better have the story *more* than perfect. Reciting alone was relatively easy, she had said, compared to a public performance. Without at least experiencing the moderately sized audience at the rehearsal, the real Equis could be perilous.

But other than my mother's warnings, Cleo seemed to have been correct. None of the elders had said anything about missing the rehearsal.

Elder Sparus met my eyes and gave me an uncertain look.

Don't think about him. Just do your best.

After having too many days filled with fourteen or more hours of intense study, I could call upon any sentence at will and have it spill perfectly from my tongue. I had pushed past the parts about the Guardian until they no longer sent chills down my spine. All uncertainties about the phrases, pronunciations, correct emphasis, and tone vanished. I even secretly recorded myself several times to listen.

I was ready.

Or so I thought. While I stared off at the spot where a treetop met the clouds, contemplating, the Equis had started.

Drums popped and boomed. Several dancers jumped and twirled on the stage. The boys and girls were elegant and energizing, much more captivating than a droll, hour-and-a-half-long story.

The seemingly unending field of Deoans watched passively on their pillows. Every pair of eyes gazed at the performers.

Those eyes will be upon me.

A surge of panic suddenly shot through me. I grabbed the pillow under me for fear I might flee.

Had my mother been right? Without the rehearsal, maybe I wasn't ready. I turned to my father to ask—no, insist—that my mother tell the story. What did it matter? I wouldn't be selected as Lead Storyteller, so why bother doing this? He winked at me and stepped onto the stage.

I called to my mother, who sat a few seats away, but only a hoarse, incoherent whisper escaped. My lungs had frozen up.

Why was Elder Sparus glaring at me?

"Well," my father said to the crowd, "before the main event—anointing Quickleaf Deo to the council—we are very excited this year to have Giels tell *The Sun and Moons*. He's, well, worked extremely hard on it, I can attest. I won't keep all of you in suspense by delaying with a bunch of announcements. Without any more waiting—Giels, come up here." He waved me forward, his mouth stretched in a giant, cheeky grin.

Why did my parents set me up for this?

The recitation was absurd. I wanted to have fun with my friends until I married. *Why did my parents rush? I have so much time in the future. Why now? Why are they doing this now? I hate this. I hate . . . them.*

My father stepped off the stage and patted me on my shoulder. Still offstage, I stared at him, but no words came. The entire Deo watched me.

"Go on, son."

My pounding heart drowned out my thoughts. A horrifying scream, blurred and eternal, echoed in my mind.

Something cold touched my fingertips. I glanced at them. Sweat.

I wiped my hands on my perfectly pressed, white tunic. My right hand brushed across my pants pocket underneath, where the recorder seemed to have been waiting to be noticed.

As if of its own will, my hand slid in, closed the petals to quiet it, and pressed the button, making the machine go back to the beginning of the last recording. The device did so instantly. My voice from the recorder cleared its throat in preparation for saying the entire recitation perfectly.

My hand still in my pocket, my fingers stopped the recitation. I stepped onstage and turned to the audience. I pulled the metallic petals apart to increase the volume.

I pressed the other button.

"THE SUN AND MOONS!" my voice boomed like a great spirit come to form, and I mouthed the words. After a couple of volume adjustments, the device projected my voice with confidence.

No one seemed to notice that the words emanated from my pocket. Why would they when it sounded exactly like me? Everyone stared, some with sincere interest.

Thirty minutes, then an hour passed, bringing us to the most exciting part, the one with the Guardian. The energy of the crowd perked up. It invigorated me. Unbelievably, the ruse was working. Relaxing, my shoulders finally dropped.

I automatically mouthed the story, even as my mind drifted.

My four closest friends and a boy named Berian sat nearby. They passed around a skin—probably of the Drink supplied by Berian. His parents made the best. Oh, I wanted some for myself. I only needed to push through a little longer.

"The Guardian . . ." my voice said.

Lightning flashed down somewhere in the South Neighborhood. It made me blink.

The boom will come . . . the boom will come . . . the boom—the demon's wingbeat. I will hear it.

And come it did, as the loudest possible thunder. Some in the audience cried out.

The memory and my mind's eye overtook me, stretching the Underworld across my vision—the great beast's wail pierced my ears like knives. The trees and people remained, but everything seemed to be secretly mechwork, as though the Deo had become machinery just under the surface. The phantom screams rose, echoing and reverberating across the landscape, drowning out the voice emanating from my pocket. I searched around in terror, my chest and throat vibrating. My mouth moved to perpetuate my lie.

Rivulets of sweat tickled my body. My mouth dried up. The

sensation of mechwork stayed. I needed to find my friends to gaze on something familiar, ordinary.

They sat just a few rows from the front. Meritus watched me with a half-smile; Alana's large eyes stared straight at me, focused, her hair oddly out of her face.

Do I appear normal?

Erikal smiled and looked down at the moss.

Cleo put her hand to Erikal's ear and whispered something. He laughed and nudged her. She poked his torso, her giggle rising just over the recorder's recitation.

My heart pounded. The next word in the story did not come to mind, but I found it quickly and moved my mouth.

Cleo looked down and grabbed a strand of grass, teasing Erikal's neck with it. He glanced up, catching me staring at him. He bumped her with his shoulder and waved his head towards me. Her beautiful eyes blinked at me very slowly, her attention hesitant.

Another flash of lightning. *The wingbeat will come.*

The recorder recited, but my mouth stopped. I waited for the flap of the great wing. I cannot say how long I remained that way. I looked around, lost.

Boom!

Everything—the trees, the people, and moss—felt odd, un-familiar. Sweat dripped from my eyelashes. I lost track of the story but quickly placed my hand over my unmoving mouth, something a storyteller should never do.

I've faked the recitation. I've deceived the council.

The ruse is over. I've been caught. My shame will forever tinge people's thoughts about me until I die.

A flash of lightning.

The words streamed back into my head, starting from the

recitation's beginning, quickly catching up to the recording.

My hand dropped from my mouth, and I silently talked along with myself.

As the thunder boomed, the last words of the story emitted from the device. Upon pressing the button to stop its recitation, I fell into blackness.

* * *

I had no memory of leaving the Equis stage. Where had I gone? I walked alone somewhere in the commons. My mouth was as dry as a stone in the Sun. My damn parents. "Damn them!" I shouted. "They should go to hell!" I shuddered, checking around to see if anyone heard the awful curse. Thank the Sun in the heavens—no one in sight.

"Giels!" a voice called from behind.

I startled so hard that I nearly leaped into the air.

The source of the call was unmistakable in its confidence. Erikal stood some thirty feet away. The Sunlight hit him, emphasizing his long face, deep-set eyes, and square jaw. He smiled. "I know you used your recorder."

Did he want to use it against me? Was it a threat?

He's still vying for Cleo. And after putting us all at serious risk with the council.

My patience had long gone.

Anger rose in every joint and muscle to my head like a fountain that had just been unclogged. I stomped towards him and threw a fist at his nose. His arm slapped my hand away. I nearly twirled around with the momentum. He smacked my right shoulder blade, and I stumbled forwards to regain my balance, almost flying. My skull knocked against a tree.

I fell to the ground, unsure which way was up.

"Damn!" I shouted. Pain thrummed on the side of my skull. I wiped my head, and a thin streak of blood transferred to my finger. My back arced awkwardly over a tree root.

Erikal came closer.

What was my next move? After a few deep inhales, I relented. People usually reported physical violence to the council—though no one else was in view. What remote part of the commons were we in?

"Hell!" I cursed.

"Are you hurt?"

"Do you care?" Having no better idea of what I should do, I rose, my palm pushing against the side of my head. Erikal winced, apparently confused and curious; a tremendous well of thought seemed to be churning behind his eyes.

I checked for blood on my clothes. None. "Why are you taking my girl?"

He grimaced. "Taking your girl?"

And again, I wanted to throw my fist. "I'm not naïve. You couldn't help yourself. Flirting with Cleo at the most important moment of my life."

"Cleo? I'm not—"

"Right in front of me."

"I'm not taking Cleo. She does what she—"

"Hell, you tickled each other!"

His brow furrowed as if considering a complex problem. "The story is long, and I suppose we lost ourselves. But I did not tickle her." He let out a quick laugh, which intensified my anger.

I stepped forward. My fingers balled up. "I saw you."

"As I recall, she tickled me with a piece of grass, but I don't—"

"The Sun! You know what I mean. You may not care about

yourself, but you're ruining my life. You. My good friend, Erikal. What? Did I say something to upset you? Is Serina right? Are you jealous of me becoming a storyteller—"

"Serina?"

"Which isn't going to happen, now. I froze, Erikal, thanks to you flirting with my girl. I understand. She's pretty, but—"

"Your girl?"

"That's why you wanted me on your idiotic journey. Since when are you so mindless? If you wanted to mess up my future, you didn't need to go into the cave. Or was the goal to really make me mad, just like lore's White Cloud, to make you look better? To have a journey that Cleo *had* to go on, which just happened to coincide with my rehearsal? It's not enough to tie up a tassel-goat with rope. You need to cut off its legs too?"

Erikal gave his head a terse shake as if casting off my rant. "I want to explain how we were able to go into the cave. I would've told you already, but you've been busy."

"What?" I had no idea what he meant. I knew how we went into the cave. I was there.

"The journey has nothing to do with messing you up. At my workshop, I can show you. It'll explain your recorder. Does anyone else know about it?"

I pressed a hand to my head. "No."

"Good. It was beautifully convincing."

"I stopped moving my mouth in the middle of it," I said, teeth clenched.

He waved a hand. "No one else'll figure it out. How would they?"

After flirting with Cleo in front of me, he's going to pretend he's on my side?

"Anyway," he said, "come in the morning. It'll open your

eyes. Also, my new cab's hull is assembled."

"Why the new cab?"

"Because I can," he said.

I groaned. Why couldn't my friends be normal? "What're you doing? I thought you knew we needed to let it go—forget the whole thing. You're smart, I'll give you that. You know the consequences."

"Listen," he said, "it's fine. We'll keep it between us. I can drive some others around. They'll have fun, tell everyone about it. That's it. No one would believe us anyway."

I searched for my anger, but it seemed to be dissipating. "Great," was all I found. By which I meant, *Leave me alone.* The pounding in my head worsened.

"Great," he said, missing or willfully ignoring my tone. "I'll see you in the morning." He walked away.

Before disappearing into the trees, he shouted back, "Cleo's thrilled you came with us. She keeps talking about it. You should go see her at the camp."

* * *

Sometime that evening, my parents opened the door to my room, waking me.

"Still tired, understandably," my mother said. "But we are letting you know that the Storyteller advisers to the council liked how your voice seemed both calm and loud. It was an unusual way of projecting, but pleasant."

"Did you need to wake me?" I said in a tired, rough voice.

My mother's head tilted to one side. "Do you not remember? You asked me to when I helped you off the stage—to tell you what the council said."

I did?

My father stepped forward. "The council still has a lot of concerns about you missing the rehearsal. You froze before the recitation and, well, honestly, your body shook a bit during that last part, not to mention you covered your mouth. We're all glad you are well, but after you fell—"

"What are you saying?"

"The advisers may believe you have . . . recitation nerves," my mother said in her most careful tone.

Of course. Nerves. Who wouldn't their first time in front of thousands of people? "So what? I'll get used to it." I wished they wouldn't bother me about it. Not then. My head still hurt, my heart weighed in my chest like a rock, and I could barely keep my sleep-deprived eyes open.

My father cleared his throat as though preparing to say something delicately. I rolled over to look away. "Uh, Giels," he said, "the council insists on having the highest standards and utmost care in selecting Storytellers, and especially the Lead Storyteller, of course."

A jolt of fear hit me. I'd expected the news, but I didn't want to hear it. I preempted them. "They've rejected me, I know."

"Actually," my mother said, "they want you to recite at the Subennial. They were so impressed with your vocal projection and clarity that they want to give you another chance." My head snapped back to face her. I stared, shocked. In return, her mouth spread into a huge grin.

My body went limp from exhaustion, every muscle worn heavy. It would mean another three months of intensive study— more intensive than the last four, as the Early Subennial stories were longer and much more complex than *The Sun and Moons*. None rhymed at all for some unknown reason.

How did the council not reject me? A part of me, the exhausted part, wished they had. I had not come close to Lead Storyteller perfection.

Or had Cleo been right all along? Did the council find an excuse to give me—to give the son of their leader—another chance? Could I not fail? If they only knew that I had cheated, that I struggled to believe the lore. I didn't deserve it.

"Which story do they want me to recite at the Subennial?" I asked, trying to show some semblance of interest.

"It is the longest one," she said, "but is also the most exciting story of the ceremony. You are familiar with it, of course. *White Cloud's Fall*—a man's slow destruction and descent to madness after his encounter with the Guardian." Her broad grin remained on her face.

My eyes rolled, and my head rolled with them into the pillow. "Oh, the Sun."

Oh, hell.

4

Secret Knowledge

My eyes blinked open to my dim room. The Sun had not yet risen from his travels under Dayodec, the earth-mother.

Pressing my fingers to the side of my head, I found that the sharp pain had gone.

Erikal had me curious about how he made my recorder. My father had been suspicious of his inventions, and perhaps I would learn why. But what pushed me from the bed early was that finally, having no responsibilities, I would find Cleo as soon as I finished with him.

I stepped out to our garden. Stars glimmered in the clearing over our home's front entrance. The moon Emba, having just risen above the eastern horizon, peeked through the trees. The deep yellow, predawn Sunlight kissed the sky just enough that I could discern my way.

Because of the dim light, I walked along the edge of the open, mossy plain of the commons where the Deo Stream ran. I avoided the south side of the water where the landscape changed dramatically from the commons: hilly, chaotic, and thick with underbrush.

Herds of tassel-goats eyed me through their long, knotted fur as I meandered around them.

Alana entered my mind. On several occasions, I had seen her walk through the area while the Sun rose.

Within moments, like a spirit I had summoned, there she was, slowly moving about in a loose, white dress, appearing and disappearing between distant tree trunks.

"Hey, friend!" I called.

She turned and, smiling, hastened my way.

Alana tied her hair back, which brought her round, moon eyes into full view. "It's a little early for most."

"Erikal wants to show me something about something. I was up anyhow."

Her expression turned cockeyed, barely detectable. "Something about something? I'd rush over too."

I laughed. It felt good to do that again. "Sounds like it's going to be about the cave."

"Maybe The Dare Furthur?"

"Dare Furthur?" I asked.

"His new cab," she said. "I haven't gone to his home, but I hear it's huge."

Why did she bring up the cab? Does she believe Erikal plans to return to the cave with it? "Whatever it is, he said it'd also explain my recorder."

"Your recorder?" she said, looking off into the distance. "I was thinking about how miraculous your recordings are. So many memories find their way deep into the caves of people's minds and hide. There they wither, get old, and die, just like people. Everything dies—everything. But not in the immortal realms. Your recorder is a little piece of that."

I hadn't awakened enough to wrap my mind around what she

said, but she stared as if awaiting a response. "It's recording us now," I said to give her one. I forgot I had left it activated until then. More and more, I had it record. I saw little reason not to, as long as no one else listened.

Alana weaved her arm under mine and pulled me forward. "Let's go see something about something." I didn't mind her joining me and didn't care if Erikal would.

At a spot with stepping stones, we crossed the stream. The trail to the south threaded stands of towering oaken trees, some so thick that the windows of homes peeked out between the massive roots. The Sun's morning-yellow hue cast its long, magic shadows on the forest. Insects darted about; some of their translucent wings caught the Sunlight, glowing like faeries might. Alana held a gentle, serene smile.

My tension from the past weeks dissolved a little.

We closed in on the Deo's southernmost homes, the area where Cleo and Erikal lived.

"Have you seen Illyia?" Alana asked.

"What?"

"The camp."

"They call it Illyia?" I asked. "Like the legend?"

She nodded.

According to the legend, Illyians had caught the attention of Salihandron because of their inventiveness, and the god had allowed the tribe to walk past the end of the World. The tale didn't explain what became of the people. Unlike lore canon, the domain of precise storytellers, legends shifted and morphed from teller to teller. And, like that of Illyia, many seemed less structured, even incomplete.

"Why Illyia?" I asked. "Because of Meritus's workshop?"

"I think so. It's kind of fun. More and more go see the place.

Friends of friends. Some even live there now to help out with the inventions."

"It's worth sleeping in a tent?"

"It's not just tents. Cleo's colorful tarp lies over the eating area. She put another over the computers and producers and new machines. I could show you. It's close."

The growing interest in the place made me uneasy, mostly because Meritus had helped make yellow dye so Cleo could recreate the Underworld's yellow room. What else was going on? "Take me after we get this thing with Erikal out of the way."

Besides, Cleo might be there.

Soon, we arrived at Erikal's home. A row of fine, alabaster blocks stuck out from the side of a forested berm. Squarish decorative knots covered the stone row, and below it ran an uninterrupted wall of glass panels, with the kitchen on the other side.

Erikal's mother, Mariette TenTensen, worked in their Sunlit garden out front. His parents seldom visited the Deo proper, so it had been a long time since I had seen her—long enough that the lack of resemblance to her son hit me.

"Giels, is that you? How long has it been? You're turning into a man," Mariette said. She stopped her do-it-all, stood up, took off her gloves, and swiped at the soil on her clothes. Sturdy and tall like Erikal, she could have been a blood relation to her son. But her warm-toned skin, softer features, and deep brown eyes unmistakably showed she was one of our people, a mixture of Bael and Midlander.

People generally knew that Erikal's parents had adopted him, mostly because of his lighter and more angular features. But Erikal never talked about it, probably because a rooted Deoan lineage mattered in the Old and South Neighborhoods.

"It's good to see you. What brings you here?"

"Just Erikal." I made myself sound casual. If she knew anything about going into the cave, she wouldn't have been exchanging pleasantries.

Mariette smiled at Alana. "Who's your friend?"

"Don't you know Alana?"

"No." Mariette clasped Alana's right hand. "I don't think I've seen you. Nice to meet you."

Alana pulled locks of hair over her eyes until her face no longer showed. "Likewise," she said, almost in a whisper.

Mariette shrugged and turned back to me.

"We're here to see his new cab and maybe ride back to the Deo with him," I said to give her a plausible reason.

Mariette glanced at the sky. Her long, greying hair fell behind her head. "If the Sun and the moons themselves did not speak to the boy, I'd be surprised. Did he tell you where he wants to go in that giant?"

I shrugged, again hoping to appear casual and non-conspiratorial.

"Well," she continued, "as always, he's in the work-court."

I thanked her. We rounded the berm where the path to their home continued through a dense wood and ended at the court's entrance.

The TenTensens didn't have a typical workshop—a small room with a single computer and producer. They had a compound. Erikal had built much of it, including a large rectangular court separated from the forest on two sides by imposing sandstone block walls as if they protected great secrets beyond. In one wall stood a double gate of wood planks even taller than the stone. Such was the benefit of living in the South Neighborhood. The council decreed the homes be far apart, which allowed the extraction of more building materials for each one.

We approached the gates. They moaned with deep creaks while slowly rotating and revealing the courtyard's beautiful, white alabaster paving. At the center, rising from the Sun-soaked white plane and ringed by tools and parts, floated Erikal's new cab.

My breath escaped me. Fifteen feet at its highest, no more impressive a vehicle could have existed anywhere. It loomed with its extraordinary size, of course, but the power and sensitivity of its design dazzled my eyes more than its immensity—the subtle variation of metal alloys, the recursive patterns within patterns of the panel joints and window muntins.

Jealousy and pride surged in me at once. I both hated and loved the sight.

Erikal floated by the hull's side on a seat with wings of slowly undulating sheet metal facets. He lowered a little and jumped off. "Alana, good," he said. "Glad you came."

On two sides of the court, the facades of storage rooms, computer rooms, and his home sat under the berm. A door slid open. Erikal waved for us to follow him.

Within the dark interior, a crouched figure fidgeted with a piece of machinery. Cleo.

I winced and crossed my arms. "What're you doing here?"

She took her time placing a machine part down and turned, her full lips stretching into a smile. "All of us wake very early at Illyia, and Erikal mentioned you were probably coming by today."

At Illyia. "Oh," I said, and let out a breath. She had come because of me. *Maybe I'm being overly paranoid. Relax.*

Bright yellow craft paste covered the workroom walls, presumably Cleo's doing. The dreamlike memory rushed back. In the actual yellow room, I had jumped with excitement.

Here, counters, a computer console, stacked machine parts, and an oversized producer concealed much of the beautiful color. Still, it was astounding.

Erikal placed a palm on his large producer. A prideful smirk pushed at his cheek.

The huge machine had undoubtedly allowed him to make his vehicles' oversized wing facets and cladding panels. "Wow. Nice producer." The producer didn't really excite me, but I figured I would coax his ego, giving him what he wanted so that Cleo and I could leave. I didn't want to waste my day off from rehearsing looking at machinery.

Alana crossed her arms like me. "That's the secret to your cabs and going to the Underworld? A big producer?"

Cleo slowly ran her thin fingers along its top edge.

"No, there's more—much more," Erikal said. "This is the largest producer in the Deo. How did I design it?"

I stopped myself from rolling my eyes at his vanity. "On the computer. Listen, we all get you're good at it."

"But no one else has done it, ever. Why haven't you seen a recorder before?"

Alana laughed. "Are you going to say the computer-spirit gave you some special help?"

"You're not far off," he said. "It's the spirit's words." Erikal placed a finger on his computer's dark, titanium screen, changing its etched display of machine assemblage pictures to a chaotic image of lines, dots, and rectangles. They almost looked like a series of broken or poorly designed ladders. "This," he said, "is the computer-spirit's language."

Language? His term made no sense. "Spirits talk wordlessly,"

I said. "That's just . . . geometry."

"In fact, these shapes talk," Erikal said, his smirk widening to a full grin. "I'll start at the beginning. About a year ago, I wanted to create a stronger hammer device for a do-it-all. I had added the standard hammer drive and tried to increase its torque power. Still, it didn't work, of course." He looked at me expectantly, but I hardly understood a word. "Anyhow, I tried modifying other items, hybridizing devices, resetting defaults, hoping something would result in a larger drive. It wouldn't allow it. Instead, it invoked this display. I experimented more, and the display appeared again and again. I figured out it appears any time I attempt something not allowed by the computer, but only if I try more than once and the second try has a minor variation." With his eyebrows raised, he seemed to expect a reaction once more. I had none.

"So?" Alana asked.

"So, I thought my best option might be to look more closely at the shapes." He tapped the screen.

"Makes sense," I said, pretending to follow along. I hoped to quicken his explanation so Cleo and I could take a walk.

"Could those shapes be the spirit getting frustrated? Giving up and throwing up its hands?" Alana asked, throwing her own hands in the air.

Erikal shrugged. "That crossed my mind, but I wanted to find out for certain. For a month, I did nothing but analyze these shapes. I pushed the design limits for the five main categories of hammer drives so that the spirit's language would appear on all. I noticed a pattern. The lower right of the screen always contained a similar arrangement—if I worked on a hammer drive, that is. The same was true for any category of device. The lower right was the same for all designs in the same category but different from category to category. In chalk, I copied each pattern on the floor so I could compare—"

"You did what?" I said. The council only allowed themselves to possess chalk, but few knew why. I knew only because, as a child, I had watched the shamans use sticks of it while I hid behind our courtyard statue of Tohillocen. During the private ceremony, they traced odd geometric figures on the flagstone paving.

Chalky remnants covered Erikal's entire floor. He had broken yet another sacred rule. It seemed like everything my friend did these days upset me. Maybe breaking the rules was in his foreign blood. "How did you find chalk?"

"It doesn't matter," Cleo said. "Just listen."

Her words hit like a quick smack. I clamped my teeth and feigned patience.

Erikal cleared his throat. "The more similar the hammer drive design, the more similar the shapes on other parts of the screen." He walked over to a shelf holding hammer drives of various sizes and picked one up. "This is the only hammer drive *not* used in a do-it-all that's the same diameter. And, I found a portion of the display where the shapes were the same as for the do-it-all."

He looked at us as though he'd just made the most remarkable statement since the god Salihandron long ago had declared, "Mortals are free!" I glanced at Cleo. She still held her slight smile.

"Okay, maybe this is not making sense," he said, "but what it means was that the spot on the screen is something other than meaningless shapes. And this is where it gets deep. You can replace shapes with other shapes." He held his finger to the screen and tapped a couple of times, and the shape changed.

"That's it. I could shrink the size of a powerful drive to fit the do-it-all."

"You made a strong hammer drive for a do-it-all?" I asked.

Erikal's eyes flashed. "You've got it!"

I wasn't so sure I did. "Why not just ask Fairfox for help? She's pretty good with—"

"No," Cleo said. "There's no way to do it, even for Fairfox."

"Thank you," Erikal said. "That's my point. No one could've made a strong hammer drive for a do-it-all." He looked back and forth between Alana and me. "You only need to look at what you have in your pocket to believe me. I did ask Fairfox for help with that, but only because she's good with small devices, not because she can make a recorder. Recording voices is not an option, normally. Otherwise, wouldn't everyone make one? If you only knew how much experimentation that required."

"Oh, the Sun," Alana said. "Maybe you're communing with the other realms. Like the Secret Knowledge in *The Sun and Moons*. It helped you make a recorder, and go into the cave."

Erikal nodded. "The Secret Knowledge. I like that." He looked at me, glowing as if expecting me to be excited too.

I sat on a metal box. The forbidden Secret Knowledge: the knowledge of the Underworld that turned Emonu and Demobawa's three sons into the Guardian; the understanding the Guardian injected into White Cloud, turning him mad. The geometric computer display was certainly not that. Their reasoning was bizarre.

"The computer helped me discover this secret," Erikal said, glancing at Alana. "That's why your idea of Salihandron sending the message made sense to me. The spiritual realms are guiding us to something."

The Guardian is making us all mad. "Stay," the voice had said to me as I escaped from the beast, "and receive some great reward."

What if by "stay," the voice meant our minds would stay in the Underworld, even after we had left, just like White Cloud's curse? Knowing the lore, and thus knowing about the madness, perhaps I could fight it. As a man obsessed with returning and seeing things in shapes, telling him things from beyond, Erikal must have already succumbed.

I was at risk too. Certainly I had imagined the voice.

Given that with curses, words and even tone mattered, I needed to sound unaffected. I could not let myself believe I was cursed. "This doesn't mean anything, except that you're using the computer." I waved my hand as if dismissing Erikal's entire notion.

Let it destroy him, not me. The Sun, did I just think that?

Erikal stared at me a moment, wincing. "Honestly, I'm surprised at your reaction. No other computer can do this. Don't you want to know why? I do."

Cleo leaned against the producer, seemingly undaunted, as though waiting for something to click in Alana and me.

"Did you know about this?" I asked her.

Cleo nodded. "Erikal told me when I asked if there was a way to make enough yellow craft paste for an entire wall. It's how the producer made so much of it."

The yellow rooms. Oh, Cleo!

Had the curse infected her? She could not let the world of the dead go, either. "Friends. You're toying with something perilous. The camp, the yellow, the inventions—you're assuming it's good. But it's already ruining me. The council almost rejected my bid and is making me do another recitation. If I hadn't been gone on the journey, none of this—" As I talked, a fury rose from somewhere that shocked me with its strength. I feared I would take another swing at Erikal. "I need to go."

I hit the button on the wall, the door whooshed, and the room lit up from the overbearing brightness outside. A long, sheet-metal panel barred my way into the courtyard. I kicked it, and it slid across the paving, clanging and bouncing. I caught Erikal's parents staring at me through the house's glass wall. The massive gates creaked open, and I wasted no time heading for home.

"Giels!" Alana called from behind. I ignored her.

"Giels!" Her feet scuttled closer. She and all of her hair popped in front of me. "Where're you going?"

"Where am I going? What the hell is he, and she, doing?"

Alana's mouth dropped. "Watch your language!"

I groaned. "What do you want?"

"What's gotten into you?"

"What? Really? You're the one who kept reminding us of the danger of that place when we were down there."

"Is that why you're angry—because they're not afraid?"

The statement gave me pause. Yes, everything would have been different if they had been afraid, but . . . "I'm angry because Erikal is under a delusion that the computer spirit is talking to him, personally, in some language of shapes, like he's a shaman or great priest, and he's pulling Cleo in, and me, and you."

"If the language is helping him, it must mean something."

I nodded emphatically. "Right! He's going crazy. You know, it happens. Elder Daiela—have you ever talked to her? She's possessed. People get unnatural ideas, then spirits infect them permanently. I can't believe Cleo's so casual about it."

She grabbed my arms. "I understand, it's absurd—crazy, as

you say—but look at his cab. Could it make sense there's some divine reason?"

There was no possibility, none, that what Erikal had said was true—that the computer gave him special skills. I could not understand how Cleo blindly believed it, and now Alana. I certainly wouldn't allow myself to go down that dangerous path.

Believing any of it means accepting madness.

I sighed loudly to make a point. "He's very good with the computer. His conceit is getting to him. That's it. If it's a spirit, tell me how he figured that out, suddenly, after millennia? Why here, in the Deo, now? Because he's so special? I am a Deo. My father is the Lead Shaman. My mother is the Lead Storyteller. He's an abandoned orphan! The computer doesn't talk with shapes. I would know."

Alana stood, unmoving.

I had said too much, lost control. The adventure, everything, had been too intense. My eyes welled up, and a tear ran down my face. "Sorry. I didn't mean that. I don't care he's an orphan."

She wiped my tear with her thumb.

I shook my head. "But something's wrong. It's not like my best friend to know about all this and not tell me."

"Maybe because he knew you'd disapprove. But also, you've been home."

"That's never stopped her from coming to my house before. She tells me everything."

"Oh, you mean Cleo? Is she what's gotten you upset?"

I pulled away and started walking.

"Since when is Cleo your best friend?" She again scuttled behind me.

"She's always been my best friend."

"Sorry. I couldn't tell."

I stopped and pressed my eyelids closed. "You don't know us very well. It wasn't me who kissed her. She kissed me first. I didn't even think of her that way." *And now she's grown beautiful.* My cheeks turned hot. I wished I would stop talking.

"She kissed you?" Alana's face screwed up. "When?"

"I— I don't know. Two years ago, three?"

Alana's shoulders dropped, head turned aside, hair cascading before her face like a black waterfall. Little more than her lips and the glint of her eyes remained visible. Those eyes sparkled, and her lips stretched. She stepped up to me. "Three years ago?" She shook her hair aside, revealing skepticism on her face.

"Yeah. So?"

"Here's what I think of her three-year-old kiss." She put her hand on the back of my neck and pulled my face towards hers. Her full lips pressed against mine. They caressed for a moment. She opened her mouth, and I opened mine. Her tongue slid over mine and up to my palette. My entire body surged as though it could fall apart. But I stood like a statue. After a few long seconds, she pulled back.

"Alana?"

The fire of Mount Saris entered my mind. When I was little, it had been only a tall peak in the distance, but now, older, I saw its beauty and understood its fiery ferocity. Alana's eyes looked up at me, and suddenly, like that mountain, I noticed something intense within her.

"I'll be honest," she said. "Your reaction is better than I expected."

"Why did you . . ."

She bit her lip, raised her eyebrows, and stared up at me with her moon eyes. She talked in a sweet, soft voice. "This may sound very odd to you, but I'm trying to help. You need to relax and have some perspective."

Perspective? I had nothing to say. In fact, I didn't understand what the kiss had to do with anything. We stared at each other in silence. Seemingly satisfied, she pulled at my hand and led me back toward Erikal's work court.

"I like Cleo a lot," she said. "She's amazing. Please don't tell her."

"I won't."

We had been far enough into the forest to be out of view of the house, but as we approached, Cleo and Erikal stood by the court's open gates. "Everything okay?" Cleo asked.

Suddenly, I felt as though I had betrayed her—not because Alana had kissed me, but because I didn't mind she had.

"We talked," Alana said as she pulled me past the opening. She continued to pull me into the work court and back into the yellow computer room, and Erikal and Cleo followed. The door slid shut. My eyes struggled to adjust to the artificial light.

At that point, I just wanted to be home.

"You certain everything's okay?" Cleo said, giving me a side glance. "What happened? Poor Giels, you look pale."

Alana jumped up and landed her rear on a counter as though she embodied new confidence. "Giels has been through a lot. I told him he needs to see things a little differently—to see new . . . ideas." She stared into my eyes. "You inspired me to go into the yellow room. Spirits frighten me, probably beyond what you can imagine. I worry one cannot both contact spirits and live. But I'm trying to be brave, partially thanks to you. You know lore and its warnings more than anyone, and you went in the room and through the door. If Erikal wants to explain how we were able to get there, don't you want to hear it?"

My head spun. I moved my eyes from Erikal to Cleo and back to Erikal. I could not get past that a girl had just kissed me, and only she and I knew it. I tried to nullify my facial expression—excitement, embarrassment. I needed to return to the discussion.

I glared at Erikal. "My father asked how you could've made the Silver Dare. He suspects something, and he doesn't seem happy. He didn't want me to ride in your vehicle at all."

The three of them stared at me as if taken aback.

"I'm not going to say anything now, don't worry—nor am I going to add deceiving the council to my list of problems." *Even though I already have.* "We are in major, major jeopardy from going into the cave. Just hope they don't press us, press me, about the trip. Stop the camp, the yellow, the large vehicles, and definitely stop with the chalk and this . . . spirit language, and maybe the council will never know." I turned to Alana. "Do you want to go?"

Alana jumped down off the counter and grabbed my hand. "Yes." Her cheeks turned red. We left with our hands clasped together. I felt Cleo's eyes following us as we exited into the Sunshine.

I was not exactly sure why I had asked Alana to join me. Perhaps I did so out of spite for Cleo not telling me about Erikal's supposed Secret Knowledge. Probably. Though maybe I just wanted the doe-eyed girl jealous.

5

Interlude in Giels

I stretched out on the courtyard floor. The fieldstone had lost its morning chill. Dappled light graced the fountain's top as the Sun made his way to the sky's apex.

No thoughts of Erikal's Secret Knowledge entered my mind. Or, I should say, I tried not to let them. The second day after the Equis was also a break: no Erikal, no stories, no adventures, no cabs, no camp, no Alana, no . . . Cleo, not even Cleo. I wanted as much time as possible to push away the entire World. An eternity? Would that mean death, a return to the Underworld?

I chuckled at the irony.

All that I was merged, mixed, and melted in my mind. Free from people and expectations, my mind was louder and more present than ever. But in its immaterial maneuvering, aspects of my life swirled in a meaningless haze—images, feelings, words. It would not congeal into a whole, clear picture. Worse, something dark, like the most stagnant pools of the Rambles, lay beneath it all.

When I pushed past Cleo's pretty face, Erikal's computer, and the myriad of churning distractions, with my arm outstretched, my fingers only tickled the calm, black water below, causing it to ripple, distorting my obsidian reflection.

My tired reflection.

Nothing existed in the black water. I wanted to dive in but feared I would search in it as obsessively as I had studied for the Equis until I drowned.

Nothing existed there, yet I played in my mind like a child with a shaman doll, telling myself that beyond my stew of problems and uncertainties, a drink lay in that pool, not stagnant and wanting, but rich and filling.

I blinked. The Sun rested directly above. Who was I that I had these bizarre thoughts? *Oh, Sun, are you talking to me?*

* * *

My mother started my practicing the following morning, and we continued the next morning, and on.

We studied as we did for the Equis, day after day.

After two weeks of grueling work, I finally had another break, but this time only until mid-afternoon while she met with her top storytellers.

Once again, my mind was free to think, though I started to dread my meditations.

The clouds puffed along through the bright blue sky above our courtyard, and in them, I saw the shapes of Underworld gods.

Nearby, our ancient, magical Billincen Device rested on its stone plinth. It tapped over the fountain's soft murmur, interrupting the calm. *Thank you, Billincen.* The pointless, annoying sound at least distracted me from ruminating on the terror of *White Cloud's Fall.*

The day at Erikal's workshop returned. I had not recovered

from it: Alana's kiss, spirit languages, yellow, looming madness. Life no longer was a day-to-day affair, but some puzzle, like a maze where the more I saw, the further I went, the more lost I became. Lore made no sense. The Underworld made no sense. My friends made no sense. Even the council and my father—

"Son," the Lead Elder's voice boomed. He stood in the courtyard by an open panel in the glass wall. I hoped to appear bored so that he'd lose interest in chatting. I wanted my peace.

He held his arms crossed like he possessed a rigid power, but the rest of him slumped, betraying the stern charade. "Your mother says studying's going pretty well."

"Yes."

"It may seem strange to bother you about this now, with you so busy and whatnot"—he paused—"but I need to ask."

Forget the bumbling. Just ask.

"Well," he continued, "I hear Erikal's building a cab larger than his last one."

My whole body tensed, but I tried to counteract it with disinterested, half-closed eyes. "True." *Don't ask any more, father. Do both of us a favor and don't ask where I went.* After using the recorder for my recitation, I couldn't stomach deceiving the council again. I might not get away with it. Time seemed to slow as I waited for his next question.

"Uh." He hesitated, looking up at the sky. He stood straight now, his arms crossed tighter than before. "That's what I thought. Just . . . focus on your studying. Stay here at home, and all will be fine, understand?"

I nodded. He turned and exited into the living area.

With a slow exhale, I stretched myself on the stone. I hadn't realized how tense I had become. Eventually, the Billincen's tapping drifted to the periphery of my thoughts. Both the Guardian and the hero of *White Cloud's Fall* now appeared in the clouds.

The ground seemed to give way, and I fell deep into the earth. *Don't be afraid. I'm imagining this.* How long could I have borne the vertigo? I fell faster. Darkness enveloped me to the point of nothingness. The mechanized Underworld appeared, unlike anything from the story I memorized. Like roots working through solid rock, terror cracked the solidity of my psyche.

The tapping sound brought me back from the vision.

I sat up, gasping. My heart raced, yet all was normal. The fountain's water still poured from its bowl in Tohillocen's hands to the pool at her feet.

The journey through the cave had driven me inward into strange visions. I feared those visions would lead to madness, and wanted them gone. Despite pushing thoughts of the Underworld away, I could not escape. It was as though some long, scaly creature writhed in the dark, deep water of my mind, pulling me in, cursing my thoughts. The more I hid from devilish notions, the more it scratched at me. The more I shoved away Erikal's Secret Knowledge, the Guardian, the yellow rooms, the messages, the more the eel-like basilisk slithered at my feet.

All of it had the opposite effect on my friends. As I drew inside to protect myself, they wanted to manifest our experience outwardly, with Erikal's cabs, Illyia, the yellow walls. It elated them; it made them feel full and freed.

Which of us was cursed?

If I understood what possessed my friends, maybe I'd better understand what possessed me. I had not gone with Alana to Illyia after leaving Erikal's workshop, preferring to return home alone.

So I stood, resolving to go to the camp today and get an answer, any answer. One answer—I'd start there.

As I rushed to get my walking shoes in the entry passage, I nearly ran into Elder Sparus. He stood in his loose, white robe, like a ghost, each hand in the other's sleeve. I stopped as though I'd hit a concrete wall.

"Ah, Giels. How are we?"

"Elder Sparus, with all due respect, I don't have many breaks, and I really—"

"Still a little tense, I see. Is something clawing at you?" He smiled.

I was about to say *no*, but didn't. Would that have been deception? Without responding, I worked my way around him sideways in the little bit of space between him and the passage wall. The odd man didn't move. He didn't even turn his head. Nor did I look back as I sprinted away.

From the path leading to Erikal and Cleo's home, I ducked into the forest. After a short way on a game trail, numerous tents, each a solid color—red, blue, green, purple—materialized through the trees and dense underbrush. The camp had many more tents than I had imagined.

My mother would want to resume our studying when she returned home. I needed to work fast.

Farther in, Cleo's polychromatic tarp hung like a hip-roof over several tables. Vibrant, dyed shapes ornamented the tarp— some wavy like streams, others like leaves or round stones. A larger, beige tarp hung over an area with computers, producers, and piles of machine parts.

The pungent scent of searing grain cakes wafted from a flame grill.

Several individuals sat on pillows under Illyia's colorful main tarp, but of them, I only knew Fairfox. None of the adventurers were there. I stood some distance away, concealed by foliage, and debated if I should find Cleo or Erikal or join this group to tease out what had brought them to live in this rough, dirty place.

Fairfox stood and disappeared into the forest understory, giving me a third option. She had helped build my recorder. She had asked Cleo to make her bedroom yellow. She was clearly as caught up in this as anyone.

I worked my way between tents and underbrush to follow, but lost her along the way. Just as I turned to trace my steps back, her colorful blouse and mantle hugging her tiny frame crossed my vision.

She slipped into a yellow tent.

"Fairfox."

"Giels? What are you doing here? Come in."

Inside, Fairfox sat cross-legged on white blankets covered in simple blue lines and knots. She glanced up and returned to patiently disassembling a small device. I sat down across from her.

She shook her thick mane from her face. Like Alana and Meritus, she had the near-black, wavy hair of the oldest tribal bloodlines of the East Neighborhood. She quickly cinched it up in two tails on either side of her head. "What're you doing here? Just wandering?"

I pulled the recorder from my pocket. "You helped Erikal make this."

Her eyes widened, and she grabbed the machine with the tips of her fingers, yanking it from me.

"I helped a little," she said, and rolled the recorder in her palm. She leaned in close, as if entranced. "I haven't seen it completed."

"You know how he did it?"

Her eyes shot up and narrowed. "Yes. Do you?"

I gave a single, slow nod to suggest I knew the secret. I wanted to say that Erikal imagined some language within a screen of geometric nonsense, but I was there to understand the camp and its draw, not refute my friend.

"Then more people know of the language," she said. "He's very protective about it. But you're a good friend and one of the Five. So, I understand."

"The Five?"

"Those who went on the spirit-journey."

Does she still believe it was just spiritual? I searched her eyes and face but saw nothing revealing, though admittedly, I was not great at reading people.

I chose my words carefully so as not to push too hard. I didn't want to give away too much, and perhaps she didn't, either. "You were not on the 'spiritual' journey." I glanced notably at her clothes and the tent. "Yet, you are as inspired by it."

Her head tilted to the side, and her eyes squinted again. "And you did go, yet you hide at home."

"Right," I said. She sounded as though she was accusing me of something, but she reinforced what I wanted to understand. Why, as I tried to live a proper Deoan life, did I grow more miserable? She and my friends gleefully shirked the Deo and broke the rules.

"I knew about the Secret Knowledge, as Erikal has started calling it, before you," she said. "I'm not sure why I was not invited on the journey. I suppose Erikal and I aren't— weren't—very close. I just helped with the recorder for a few hours."

She shrugged and returned my device. "I'll go on the next one."

I quickly pocketed the recorder. "There won't be a next one."

"No? Why do you think you can say that?"

"Why do you wear Cleo's designs?"

A shadow crossed Fairfox's heart-shaped face. "You're after something. If you want to know why I'm living here in Illyia in these clothes, just ask."

I raised my eyebrows, which I intended as a way of asking.

Fairfox's eyes hardened. "It's not just the journey," she said, crossing her arms. "It's that Erikal is being called. We don't know why, but no one else—no other computer can do what his can. The Secret Knowledge is divine. It's powerful and infectious. When something is on your mind so much, you need to do something—something, don't you?—or your mind starts to burst."

It sounded like she believed Erikal's rhetoric to the core. "Why not just do what he does without the Secret Knowledge?"

Fairfox's mouth dropped, and she shook her head. "That's . . ." Her voice edged higher than normal. "That's the question of someone who just makes everyday tools on the computer. I would've thought you knew more, being a Deo." She chewed at a nail for a while.

I waited.

A huff escaped between the girl's perfect teeth. "Not sure how to say it. There are patterns. When there's a clear pattern, you know it's what the computer wants, like in the North Neighborhood where all homes are completely underground with a sunken courtyard. I haven't designed a house, but you obviously can't design one there without a garden fully surrounding the courtyard. Probably the gardens are not just gardens, but also warnings. People know there's a hole and don't drive into the courts. Ever see one of the unoccupied homes there? After the garden dies? They don't work. Nothing in the home works. If you don't follow the design pattern and maintain it, it only takes a couple years for the home to return to soil."

I had seen such houses, where earth started washing in with the storms. After a time, it would be as if they had never been there.

"Erikal's computer," she added, "could probably design a home without a garden at all."

Every home had a computer, a manifestation of the computer-spirit, and a producer, which together helped us create everything. But the notion that the computer-spirit had that much involvement with our designs, greatly limiting what we could do and how we could do it, astounded me. I supposed I had some awareness of that, as people talked about the spirit's wisdom, but nothing so stark.

Fairfox had given me my one answer about Illyia. Whether true or not, Erikal had convinced the camp they could make what otherwise could not be made.

"Honestly," I said, "I didn't think the knowledge was anything, just meaningless shapes, like a glitch. But you're suggesting they have meaning, like—" *Like secret shamans' symbols*, I was about to say. I could not resist asking what I fundamentally wanted to understand. "You believe it's real?"

"If something is true, isn't it better to accept it?"

* * *

The next several weeks dragged by. When practicing some portions of *White Cloud's Fall*, every word felt like a little razor cut on my tongue. One part in particular:

> *Years had passed since the beast searched White Cloud's eyes. The Guardian's eyes, black as night, had swirled with the Knowledge. The forbidden colors danced in the demon's gaze. The colors danced in White Cloud's head. Thereafter, ideas of the Underworld tinged White Cloud's mind. His memories churned and meshed into tangled images. Their movement sped, polychromatic and flashing.*
>
> *He remembered fighting monsters in his home at night with root vegetables while his friends watched. He wore nightclothes all day. His friends' pupils looked large, empty, black, and judging, and stared even when he battled demons alone.*
>
> *White Cloud recoiled in horror at his reflection in the sink water. He had been an embarrassment, a failure, and saw that his heroics and quest for the truth had been farces. He realized others saw something much different than what he saw in his reflection. He realized he had gone mad.*

Every time I recited it with my mother, the swirling colors of madness, like Cleo's clothes, invaded my mind's eye. I fumbled through the words, and my mother noticed. And her noticing seemed to reinforce my insanity.

One morning I stood up and walked out on her, saying only, "I know enough. I'm going to rehearse in the woods." By "the woods," I meant Illyia. And by "I know enough," I meant that I had secretly recorded my mother telling the story. I had been home too long, and felt as trapped as I had when rehearsing the Equis—worse, I lost control of my own thoughts. I couldn't hold still. I couldn't stay at home. This time, thanks to the recorder and the camp, I had another option.

Almost as soon as I arrived at the Illyia, Cleo orchestrated the creation of a tent for me, dyed green. "Sorry it's not yellow," she said, "but we can't find snails right now." The entire time, her doe eyes sparkled.

She quickly returned to her camp work, whatever that was, and I saw little of her after.

It didn't matter. I needed to stay focused in my green tent. As I was one of the Five, other Illyians brought me food, serving wear, cleaning wipes, and other useful items. I quickly learned I was special—or maybe they assumed I needed help. In all, being at Illyia was beneficial. My thoughts haunted me less. Being around people who enjoyed ideas I considered insane actually helped.

In the month approaching the rehearsal, Illyia had weekly evening celebrations they called reveries, each having progressively louder drumming than the last. On those nights, I escaped to my bedroom at home. Usually, my mother insisted I demonstrate that my recitation was improving. My ability to study on my own astounded her.

One evening while in my bed, perhaps as a way to torment myself, I pressed the recorder's button and listened to the message that had started all of my problems. It was the first time since returning from the Wind Cave. I shifted on my pillow from hearing the unearthly voice.

Next, I would hear myself talking to Cleo at a time when nothing except the recorder seemed out of the ordinary. But I did not talk. Instead of my own, a deep, breathy voice emanated from the device. It recited the same words in the same ethereal voice that I'd heard in my head when fleeing the Guardian:

"Lost souls remain in your Underworld. Stay. They cry out for you. Stay, and you'll receive some great reward."

With a shaking hand, I deactivated the recorder and set it down. I stared at the ceiling for a long time; the subtle concrete patterns now strangely stood out in bas-relief. The shades of grey seemed to turn to reds, purples, and blues.

Perhaps denial pushes one to madness. As Fairfox said: *If something is true, isn't it better to accept it?* Maybe Meritus's blind acceptance of everything protected him like a superpower.

Was that the Guardian's technique? Seeing the horrid thing made mortals wish they could unsee it, forcing them to battle the memory to the point of hysteria?

Like an animal caught in the jaws of a greater creature, I gave up the fight.

My muscles relaxed one by one. Why or how the second message invaded my device did not matter. What mattered was, just like that, I could no longer deny I'd heard it. The initial shock faded, and relief washed over me in waves.

Some divine force needs me to understand.

For the first time since the Wind Cave, I felt sane.

6

Lightning Leads the Way

"Cleo's busy. Can I walk you?" Alana had just entered my tent, dressed not in Cleo's garments like much of Illyia's population, but a black dress and black sweater. She kneeled in front of me.

I stuffed my recorder into my pocket. "Walk me where?"

Her smile stretched wide, and she chuckled. "Stop pretending. Get dressed and come on." She stepped outside and extended her hand into the tent. "And bring a fleece. It's chilly."

Unbelievable. How did I forget?

Uncertain whether she could see me through the flap, I rushed into my performance clothes, white with red stripes on the arms and knotted red lines on the chest, which had hung patiently for a month.

We held hands the entire way to the Subennial rehearsal stage in the commons. It didn't seem odd or suggestive to hold her hand—just a friendly gesture.

Perhaps it was nerves, but another kiss would have been nice. Apparently, she had the same thought. Once we arrived, she gave me one, half on my cheek and half on my lips—a peck of encouragement, nothing more. "For luck," she said. "But I doubt you'll need it."

"Thank you." My voice broke. I put my hand to my mouth as though I could retroactively hide the nervousness.

She stared, and I detected sadness in her oversized eyes. I didn't ask. I'd grown used to her little idiosyncrasies.

"Forget about everyone else. Just tell the story to me," she said.

Though I was grateful for Alana's encouragement, I wished Cleo had walked with me. As if from a dark spell of estrangement, my studies held me back from pursuing her, and she seldom came to my tent.

An enormous boom sent a jolt through my body. Thunder rolled and rumbled in the air. "Every time I recite!"

Alana rubbed my arm. "You'll be fine."

I have told the entire story many times, perfectly. I will not need my recorder. I will not deceive again. I will not let the crowd unnerve me. And, looking at Alana, I can recite to one person.

Alana sat close to the stage. I joined the storytellers and shamans to the side of it. I smiled at my parents to project confidence, and they smiled back, a little uncertain. It surprised me. True, my mother hadn't helped me recently, but I had recited a few times for her, correctly.

A line of cabs from Illyia floated by the seating area and parked. Cleo, Erikal, Meritus, and an Illyian entourage emerged from the vehicles. Wearing their bright Illyian clothes, they snaked through the seating area and joined Alana: one girl in black surrounded by a chorus of color, surrounded by a smattering of other Deoans in simple tan or brown with striped accents.

With glances, whispers, and subtle pointing, many came close to openly gawking at the colorful gaggle of youths.

Appearance aside, my friends paid me a massive compliment

by bringing so many with them. Despite their feverish focus on inventions, they still had me in their thoughts, including Cleo.

After my father's introductory statement, the shamans began reciting a prayer, which meant it would be my turn in moments. My father nodded to me. I took a breath and walked onto the stage, faced the modest audience, and bowed.

In a couple of hours, I will be the future Lead Storyteller.

After I passed out at the Equis, my mother had trained me to breathe slowly and ease into it. If I could deliver the first two minutes confidently, the rest would flow.

In only two minutes . . .

My body vibrated. Sweat beaded on my forehead. The faces watched me; they saw my every move, my every imperfection. My hand slid into my pocket and grabbed the recorder.

I only need to press the button.

Lightning struck a tree near the back of the audience. I convulsed. Several audience members screamed.

The shock of it must have reset my nerves anew. I had gained hold of myself. I took in a deep breath, deactivated and let go of the recorder, and smiled.

The words flowed. And, soon, so did the rain. The wind blew, the raindrops assaulting my face. Perhaps Tohillocen meant to bless me.

Storytellers didn't stop their sacred stories just because of the weather.

Another bolt of lightning struck down, this time nearly hitting the gathering. Screams rang out in it its wake.

Some darted from their pillows, covering their heads.

I talked louder so that the remaining people could hear over the ever-increasing downpour. Lighting rolled across the clouds with threatening booms and static pops.

The Guardian flashed through my mind. Undaunted, I pushed the demon away. *Leave me. Keep your realm to yourself.*

More than two minutes had passed. *It'll flow naturally now. I've done it.*

The wind blew rainwater into my mouth as I recited. My eyes refused to stay open. The elders would forgive me if I cleared them with the backs of my hands. Over and over, I wiped my eyes. I pulled up the collar of my shirt and wiped them with that.

As I pushed my dripping hair from my face, I caught a glimpse of the shamans. Several apprentices had raised a cloth shelter over the agitated council.

The cold saturated me, making me shiver, making my voice break, but I adjusted my tone. My pace quickened. It was not intentional, but I noticed it, and I slowed more than I should have—too much variability. I regained my tempo. *I will not use my recorder. I know the story. I know how to recite.*

Lightning bolts flashed across the sky and hit the ground, one after the other, as though Tohillocen's sister Elloa rejected Etargoren for a second time, and he wanted the World to know his misery.

I imagined myself as some great being and held steady, determined to recite each word as it was meant to be, ignoring the rain, my stinging eyes, the water pouring into and out of my mouth, and my shaking limbs.

Distant trees disappeared in the grey haze of rainwater. Fields of yellow and white light flashed, their sources concealed in the veil, as though I were hiding under a blanket.

I stiffened my posture and projected my voice—until the last word.

Bracing myself against the cold, I rushed to sit between Cleo and Erikal who were soaked and sitting among the tightly packed Illyians under one of several tarps the apprentices had raised for the audience. I laughed at the sky, at the storm. What else was there to do?

The two of them patted me, filling my chest with reverie. I felt huge and light. I had recited every word under impossible circumstances. And, my friends had stayed.

I had never seen a storm so bad in the Deo, worse even than the one on our journey. Water had saturated the mossy ground so completely that a thin layer pooled above it, bouncing and bobbing with the rain that blew under the shelter.

Lightning bolts now shot down even more frequently. I lifted my feet to the top of the waterproof pillow below me.

Cleo took off her watertight bucket hat to offer it, revealing a simple, brass headband underneath with an odd shape sticking up at its front.

Astounded, I caressed the piece of jewelry. Recorders weren't the only legendary object that we had a word for. *Model* could mean a precise miniature version of something. "The wingless cab that frightened the Guardian."

She put her hand on my shoulder. "With Erikal's computer, we've made a new computer that has the language. With it, I made this."

"Erikal," my father shouted, "please come up here if you would." The boy did as my father asked.

The electric storm seemed to jolt inside me. "That's odd."

Meritus had been sitting on the other side of Erikal. He leaned in and talked just above the rain, "The council summoned Erikal. That's why we're here."

That's why?

Had the council discovered his secret? Would they shame him

in public? Would they mention us?

". . . with hopes that you will ascend to the highest of understanding and positions," my father proclaimed over the thunder.

Highest of understanding and positions? I knew that phrase. The realization unfolded as to why they had summoned my friend. But it couldn't be. It made no sense.

They're making Erikal a shaman.

"At the actual ceremony," my father shouted to Erikal, "you'll be sitting next to the council."

Before I realized it, I was standing.

The befuddled group of Illyians broke into chatter.

Erikal looked dizzied, but his eyes gleamed. My father gave him more instructions and congratulations while his heavy-set figure wildly gestured along with his words.

Cleo stared intently with a combination of shock and pride on her face. Alana looked at me; crooked tendrils of her wet hair framed her distress.

She had looked at me like that earlier.

"You knew?" I asked.

Alana shook her head. "I only suspected."

I meandered around the soaked audience, then walked home. Throwing myself into bed, I stared at the ceiling, trying to make sense of the day.

* * *

The house's main door slid open, followed by heavy footfalls. I slapped my door's open button and burst into the main living area. My father stood by one of the glass walls, soaked and looking out into the courtyard. The Billincen Device ticked on a cabinet nearby.

"Why didn't you tell me?" I asked. The anger in my voice surprised me.

"Well, you know shaman namings are an honor and a surprise."

"Surprise? Rumors always spread beforehand, and you usually tell me before the rumors even reach me. He hasn't ever trained. Samsen is obsessive about his training; if you're looking for another young person like cousin Quickleaf, he's an easy choice."

My father hadn't wanted me to be a shaman, which was fine, I supposed, on its own. But why, after not even attempting to train me, did he anoint my friend, who had no bloodline, training, anything—a person who forced his friends into the Wind Cave and secretly used symbols on his computer?

It felt like a slap, and a hard one because my father had kept it secret.

"The Council of Seven Elders has decided. We don't choose lightly; you know that. And I would have told you . . . if I could, but it's— I just could not. You . . . you seem upset."

"You're talking like I'm an average Deoan. I'm your son. You've always told me. Did you not want my reaction? I think, like most people, you overestimate Erikal's abilities." My words surprised me. "I could have told you some things. I know Erikal more than you and the rest of the council. What does Samsen's father think about this?"

His arms slowly moved into a tight clasp. "I promise we, including Elder Moss, made our choice very carefully."

"You didn't want me to follow you, fine, it worked out for me. But at least a Deo, or a Moss, or some other trainee with a family history."

"I see," he said, and cinched up his wet robes so he could take a seat on a pillow.

I remained standing.

My father's brow furrowed as he stared off into the court. "Giels." I knew he wanted to impart wisdom when he started a sentence with my name. "Giels," he said again, and looked down, "we need to talk about your future, but first—regarding Erikal—he's very talented, but also . . ." He paused. "This small commons that your friends have created—"

"Illyia," I interrupted.

He now stared right at me. "Yes, yes, okay. We think Erikal . . . and you pointed out that you are my son, and so I am confiding in you now, do you understand?"

"Yes, of course," I said, with a dismissive wave. "Just tell me."

"Yes, fair enough. We think Erikal is—" He tightened his furrowed brow. "Well, a little different, and—"

"I know," I said, throwing my arms up, "most people do. That's not new. He just happens to be tall and good looking or whatever and happened to stumble on some things in his computer."

"Yes, but to stumble, as you say . . . We elders have wisdom, which is held tight for very fundamental reasons. I think you know that, but whatever he stumbled upon should not be. Not unless something very, well, special is happening. Something different, something that you may not be aware of."

Was he talking about the computer's spirit language? I allowed him to think I was ignorant of it to see what he'd say. "What's happening?"

"The spirits, or something even greater," he said, shifting on his pillow.

Maybe he knew about the language. But why would it make Erikal a shaman? Cleo had said it: They'd made a replica of Erikal's computer, and she'd used it too. It was nothing special anymore.

My father searched my eyes. "What I'm saying may sound shocking. Or, does it?"

"Shocking? No. It makes no sense. You and the council just don't realize that the spirit language doesn't make him special."

My father's head tilted to the side a little as if some small, new idea came to him. "The spirit *language*? Why did you say spirit *language*?"

Oh, hell, he didn't know?

"The regular pictures of designs, on the screen," I said in hopes of hiding what I had meant. "I don't know. I thought that's what you were talking about." His eyes held their suspicious squint, so I returned to the topic at hand. "Why is there so much attention on Erikal? There aren't even any openings in the council right now. This is my day, which I fought very hard for."

We stared at each other for a moment. His eyes were red, moist, and he turned away to face the court.

"What?"

"I suppose we need to discuss that," he said, talking to the glass.

"What?"

"We decided that it's probably better—"

"What?" An electric shock hit me. "I said the entire thing perfectly despite everything."

"You didn't. Your voice didn't project like last time. It quivered. The storytellers thought it sounded . . . weak. And rushed in parts, or slow. Storms are expected this time of year, and they want perfect steadiness, despite any distractions. I'm sorry, but—"

"Weak? This was the heaviest rain, and—"

"It's the Lead Storyteller role they're judging you on."

What a bunch of tassel-goats' asses! "This isn't real, is it? You think I'm not ready and Erikal is? This recitation was your idea. I did this because of you." I grasped my recorder as though it might save me and rewind the day.

A small piece of metal hit the floor nearby and rolled across the stone paving.

My father's eyes shot in the direction of the sound. "Balance," he murmured. He glanced at my hand, which held the recorder through my clothes. "What've you got there?"

Startled, I reflexively pulled my hand up to my chin. "Nothing."

The metal continued to roll slowly. The stick on the Billincen Device, which had balanced on the pewter pyramid for generations, lay on the floor. It had never before fallen from its perch.

My father nervously scrambled to the device to arrange the stick's center back onto the pyramid, but it would not stay. He cursed under his breath, saying words like "hell" and "shit"—something my father didn't do.

Giving up on the device, he pounded his fist on the counter.

"Father?"

"What've you got there?" he demanded again, pointing at my pocket, the fat under his chin shaking. "An invention of Erikal's?"

His tone frightened me. "Father, no. What does that have to do with—"

"I told you not to go with Erikal and not to go to the camp! To stay here and practice! You disobeyed me. You believe you know what you're doing, but you don't. And you wonder why you didn't perform well."

At that comment, something in me stopped, and everything in my mind turned quiet, like a clear spring day. And, not a second later, fury replaced all reason. "You want Erikal to be a shaman, and you just give it to him. You want me to be a storyteller, and I nearly kill myself. Meanwhile, you don't want me around him? What am I?"

The storm outside seemed to enter my mind. I walked to the counter that held the annoying device's tiny pyramid and grabbed it. I hated the obnoxious, constant tapping. I suffered it only because it held meaning for them. "*You* don't know what *you're* doing. I receive messages, and you are all too blind to see that he's cheating, and I am the one!"

I'm the one. The thought echoed through my mind.

My mother stood a little distance away, watching the scene unfold. She stepped forward, looking back and forth between us.

My arm made a full rotation over my head. I released the pyramid in a concerted throw at the courtyard's glass wall. The tiny bit of metal should have done nothing to the structural glass. I meant only to make a statement.

The next moments unfurled as though time slowed. The pyramid flew, but before it hit the glass, my father leaped at me. The piece hit one of the full-height glass panes, which shattered into millions of small pieces, exploding with force into the court. My father's shoulder smashed into my chest. We flew several feet, his body pinning me to the floor. My mother screamed. The earth-retaining parapet above the broken glass gave way, along with the concrete ceiling next to it.

The concrete boomed like thunder and shattered.

Chunks, gravel, and sand rained down nearby, and the earth above rushed in, carrying entire trees into the courtyard. The artificial lights flickered off. The cloudy sky glowed through a large, jagged opening. Only the glass pane hit by the pyramid had broken. The others remained, with several feet of dirt and debris on the other side pressing against them.

The ceiling above us held.

My ribs and arms contorted under my father's weight. I tried to scuttle out, but his large body held me like a trapped animal. He pushed himself up, pressing his hand against his head. My mother called for us from beyond the wreckage.

My father rose to one knee, and I stood.

I checked my pocket for the recorder. And I fled.

7

Hold Me Up High

The black water.

I heard the voice.

If I were to dive into the stagnant swamp below all of my distractions, I feared that a creature, toothy and long, like a scaled water dragon, waited to drag me down.

I am the one. The truth stirred about, but I had hidden that phrase from myself in the black liquid, afraid of its bite. When I had said those words to my father, the creature slid from the murk and into me.

I . . . am the one.

The dragon was not a thing to fear. It was power.

The storyteller role may no longer have been a possibility, but Illyia was.

The voice in my head; the recorder Erikal had given to me, and the message within it; Cleo's insistence that I go on the journey; my failure at the rehearsal; the storm. Everything seemed to be pushing me. I only needed to wade into the dark water. I only needed to listen.

At Illyia, I was one of the Five. At Illyia, I mattered. I possessed the recorder that had started it all. I had received the message in the Underworld.

When the group of youths noticed me approaching the main tarp at Illyia, all stopped what they had been doing. The ones along my path stepped aside. A boy I did not know slightly bowed as I walked past. And another bowed, and another.

The mood was strange, thick with something I couldn't identify. I'd been there for weeks, hoping to discover what the place meant for me. But I had hidden in my tent, unthinkingly avoiding its energy, until now. I soaked it in, one aspect immediately hitting me—the drive for discovering what lay just under the surface, within the darkness.

My posture, slumped with angst, straightened. My chin raised. The horror of the argument with my father earlier and our destroyed home lifted. I needed to shove that into the deep, dark water for the moment. I wanted to focus on what the camp might give me. And what I might give it.

In fact, I wanted more. I needed my friends to help me understand the voice in my head, even if it meant returning into the depths.

Hiding flowers behind my back, I found Cleo assembling a tent.

"Giels!" she shouted. She ran up and hugged me. "I made clothes for you, but I've been so busy, I keep forgetting."

Heat rose to my cheeks as I revealed the bouquet of red flowers.

She blushed beautifully, like the fire-flower blooms I'd given her. Then she grabbed my wrist with her thumb and forefinger. "That's thoughtful on *your* day. I was worried you'd bask in your success, and I wouldn't see you."

I scoffed. "I wanted to see you. And I want to say sorry. I was in a bad way when you and Erikal told me about—"

"It's fine. You've been under strain." She pointed up. "Look, not a cloud."

"Tohillocen had it in for me, I suppose. Worst storm in years."

"The worst ever. I thought they'd tell you to pause, but you pushed through." She lightly punched my shoulder. "How do you feel?"

Everything my father had said hurt tremendously. But with the pressure to rehearse now gone, I managed to shoulder the heavy weights pulling at me. "I'm well—really well."

"You are," Cleo said, searching my eyes. "Like at peace. It's nice to see you breathe a little." She smiled. "We have a reverie tonight, a big one. Will you—" She stopped and stared past me.

I turned but saw nothing unusual, just tents and a few people milling about.

"What are the shamans doing here?" she asked.

Then I saw it—Elder Sparus's cab, with its near-black patinated copper cladding, my father sitting next to Sparus. It weaved through the brush.

I destroyed my home with the broken Billincen Device. My father suspected a machine in my pocket broke the device. He knew Erikal made it, and he was angry. Erikal made it with the Secret Knowledge, which I revealed to my father. A supposed language that could be like shamans' symbols.

I didn't know why or how it all connected, but the council might.

But no terror of our secrets being discovered came as it had before. Instead, I felt guilt and frustration. The council allowed only themselves to have any knowledge of shamans' symbols, which I'd only known about by sneaking around council meetings as a child. I've endangered my friends, the camp, and what I wanted.

Elder Sparus, being almost as good as Erikal at reading people, would easily see through lies. We were still in the same situation.

We cannot tell them. We cannot deceive them.

I dropped to all fours and placed the flowers in a nearby bucket.

Cleo raised her palms. "What under the Sun?"

"Shhh! Hide. Where are Erikal, Alana, and Meritus?"

Cleo half-hid behind a tent, watching the Elder's cab. "Don't know. Erikal's probably working."

"What's my father doing?"

"They were talking to a couple of people, but now they're leaving. Heading south. Why're we hiding?"

"I'm going to Erikal's. Find Alana and Meritus, and meet me there. And maybe Fairfox. Tell everyone not to tell the council anything. The computers, the inventions, nothing at all."

It was long past time we coordinated a plan to keep it all secret. Hopefully, before my father and Elder Sparus found out more.

Slinking, I meandered through the camp and made my way south through the thick forest underbrush. Just as Erikal's home came into view, Elder Sparus and my father exited the house, settled into the cab, and floated north on the main trail.

Dammit!

The gates of Erikal's courtyard groaned open for me. In the same yellow computer room where he had described the Secret Knowledge, Erikal sat on a stool, slightly hunched. He didn't seem panicked or angry—good. The shamans must not have spooked him.

"You really need to oil those gates," I said with a smile, wanting to start things light and coax out what had happened with my father. The conversation might get heated if he knew I had revealed the language.

Erikal forced a smile. "Hey." He picked up a small mechanical part from a counter, rotated it in his fingers, and returned it to the same spot.

"What do you think of your ascension?" A pang of jealousy hit, but I reminded myself that it should not. The voice had talked to me.

"It's fine," he said, as if unexcited by it. "I'm not surprised. I think they've considered me for a long time. My father suggested as much before we left for the Wind Cave."

"Suggested? The council didn't tell you?"

He sighed. "No, and I didn't try to find out if my father was right. Truthfully, I didn't want to think about it."

"Why?"

He looked up at his computer and producer. "I'm not ready to stop."

I threw up my arms. "I knew you weren't looking to be a shaman. This doesn't make sense."

For months, Erikal had made me angry, but now, no anger came. A part of me had wondered if Erikal asked to be a shaman to hurt me, but that seemed too contrived and insane. In fact, I wanted to console him. He rarely expressed strong emotions, but he appeared subdued to the point of despondency. "Initiates normally wait six months before observing the council. But the council doesn't have any openings. It's probably longer for you."

He glanced at me. "I have no time."

"Why not?"

"Your father and Elder Sparus came by."

Good. The topic I'd wanted to discuss. What did the council try to find out about the Secret Knowledge? I tempered the concern in my voice. I didn't want to give anything away. "What did they ask?"

"Ask? Nothing. They want me to start observing the council members immediately."

"That's all they said?"

"Isn't that enough?"

My father didn't ask him about the spirit language. Had I actually managed to deflect it? Great, but after I had destroyed our home, why had his first reaction been to tell Erikal to start early?

Now I was curious. "They didn't give you an exact day?"

"Tomorrow," Erikal said.

I pushed my hand through my hair. This could ruin what I wanted to do. "Why?"

"They didn't say. They just said it's allowed with me almost nineteen. They behaved oddly. Your father looked haunted."

The door slid open, Cleo on the other side. "Oh, good, you're both here."

Erikal let out a slow, intentional breath and gave her a meek smile.

"Are you okay?" Cleo asked. He nodded. "Elensra the Treespeaker is in your house," she said. "She asked me about the camp." Cleo looked at me. "I said nothing, but she seems suspicious. Now can you tell me what's going on?"

"Where's Alana and Meritus?" I asked.

"I couldn't find them. What's going on?"

"The Treespeaker might be worried about the trees at the camp," Erikal said. "I'll tell her the camp is temporary, and we'll dismantle it. Friends, I knew this would end someday. Our fate changed more quickly than expected, that's all." He stepped out into the Sun.

Cleo's expression shifted to a scowl. "What did you say to him?"

I folded my arms. "Me? Nothing. That's Erikal. He's upset because the council wants him to start tomorrow."

She closed her eyes and shook her head. "Sorry." Cleo leaned against the doorjamb and rubbed her face. "So, that's what's going on? They want him to start tomorrow?" The words came out in a low growl.

I didn't respond. It wasn't the reason I had asked her here, just a new complication.

Cleo's lips tightened. She folded her arms and stared outside for a while. The reality that the camp might be over seemed to be sinking into her, as it was me.

"After all we've done," she said, "after where we've gone, his ascension is going to ruin it, isn't it? It's like being closed in, and then a door opens and shuts again. We can't go on without Erikal. Meritus does what Erikal wants. Alana seems to be following what you do. I know you don't care." Her delicate face glowed red with frustration.

"Maybe I do."

"Oh, Giels, you went because I promised . . . well, you know what."

Yes, a kiss, I remember. My heart raced.

"I'm a fool. What I promised should mean something, not be a—"

"Cleo—"

Her hand pressed on my arm. "I need to tell you this." Her eyes, framed in long, deep-brown lashes, stared into mine. They welled up.

"I need to tell you something first," I said. "It's important." I took a step forward, and she retreated a step. I pressed the door's close button, and it thwapped shut, darkening the room.

Her expression soured. "Why'd you close the door?"

"So we can talk." I took another step to her.

Suddenly, I had a heightened awareness that we were alone.

She pressed her back against the door. "You know I like you. We're so close, and I wouldn't mind, you know, but—"

I moved closer, our bodies now inches apart. Heat surged to my face and my breathing deepened from being so near to her. But we were there to talk. I looked straight into her eyes so that she'd take me seriously.

"Wait," she said, "give me a chance to say something. At this time, I—"

Her body stiffened, and her eyes darted as though she wanted to escape, as though I planned to do something. But I just needed to tell her what I had heard in the Maze of Azer. "The Underworld wants us to return."

She winced. "What?"

"I heard a voice."

Her arms and shoulders dropped. "A voice? What do you mean?"

"After the Guardian flew away, when you were yelling at me to come into the yellow room, it told me that they needed help."

"They? Who?"

"Spirits, the dead, gods, I don't know. It spoke into my mind."

Her expression turned dubious. "Are you sure?"

"I'm certain. It was as clear as you talking to me now. I remember every word. And a few days ago, I heard the same voice, the same words, in my recorder." I took the device from my pocket and pressed its buttons. Starting from the beginning, it recited the original message and the new one, which matched the voice in my head.

Cleo looked up from the little machine. Her jaw dropped. "Why haven't you said anything?"

"Honestly, it put the devils' fear in me. I convinced myself I had imagined it. Until I couldn't deny it." I raised the device. "For some reason, whoever—whatever—it is, they're talking to me, and not the shamans." *And not Erikal.*

Wonder flashed in Cleo's eyes. "You know this is real, don't you?" Her voice was thick with both desperation and relief. "I've been waiting."

"Aren't you scared?"

"Yes, of course." Her eyes stared deep into each of mine.

Need and want filled those gorgeous orbs. Whether it was because of me or the voice I heard, I did not know, but at that moment, I didn't care. My persistent desire for her overwhelmed me, and I leaned in close.

Her chin lifted, mouth opened and eyelids narrowed as if swept into a dream. "I don't know what this means. But I owe it to—"

She closed the gap between our lips. I pulled her body against me. Our mouths caressed, and I took her tongue in mine. No moment had bound me in ecstasy more.

After a short while, she placed her hand on my chest, pulled her face away, and smiled. I didn't want to stop. I was light-headed, elated, and honestly, stunned. I didn't know what the kiss meant, either, or what the voice meant, but I felt us heading into some untethered unknown. There had to be a way to keep going.

"Have you ever just wanted something so much?" she asked. I nodded. Cleo smoothed her clothes and fixed her pulled-back hair. "We need to talk to Erikal."

The door whooshed open and, as if on cue, the boy's two

hundred pounds of muscle and bone rushed in, panic in his eyes.

"What happened?" Cleo said.

"How did the Treespeaker know?"

Cleo grabbed his upper arm. "Know what?"

"About the Secret Knowledge. She said that mortals should only design with pictorial diagrams and not try to speak to the computer directly." Erikal looked at me.

Dammit. I swallowed hard. In the afterglow of the kiss, I didn't want to admit to revealing the spirit language—that I might have endangered Illyia.

Erikal's brow wrinkled. He glowered at me. "What did you say?"

I must have looked like an animal in a trap.

"This is stupid," Cleo said to Erikal. "You didn't create the language. You simply figured it out. What's more shaman-like than that?"

Erikal's shoulders released their tension, and so did mine.

"Maybe you're right," Erikal said. "I can continue with it as a shaman. I might need to approach them about it carefully."

"Except, the shamans keep everything to themselves." She groaned. "Giels."

What did she want me to say?

"Yes," Erikal said, "but *I* don't need to stop." He looked around as if searching for a thought. "We went where no one else had. And shamans cannot be punished. Once I'm an elder, I can take the blame if they ever find out. Maybe this will all work out. But it probably means Illyia is done."

"Giels!" Cleo commanded.

I startled to attention, understanding what she wanted. "Right, I need to tell you something." I considered how to say it. I didn't want to insult him. He, or his vehicle rather, was now crucial to what I wanted, and I probably had only one chance at getting it. "I don't believe that you're the only one who the spirits are talking to."

He squinted at me, his expression suffused with genuine curiosity.

I described the entire moment in the Underworld when I had heard the voice in my head. I had the recorder recite the new message to prove it.

Erikal stared at me as though reading my deepest thoughts. I resisted looking away.

"I believe you," he said. "I have no choice. Adding a message at the beginning is impossible—by us, anyway." He glanced at a dark corner of the room, but his eyes twinkled as though staring at some grand vista.

I'd escaped blame from Illyia's end, for now. It was my chance to take charge.

"One more time," I said. "We should go one more time. I need to. I need to know if there's more. I don't trust the council right now. Cleo's right. They'll suck everything from you and keep it to themselves, leaving the rest of us stranded." Cleo touched my arm. I said everything she wanted. "And, I have nothing to lose anymore."

"How about Lead Storyteller?" Erikal said.

I shook my head.

Shock washed over Cleo's face. "What?"

"I've broken the line," I said. "My parents will be the first of my ancestors who have no child as either a shaman or a Lead Storyteller."

Cleo cried out and grabbed my arm.

"When would we go?" Erikal asked. "I start tomorrow."

Cleo put a hand on Erikal's chest. "It's not too late. Would anyone else know you're supposed to start tomorrow? The council won't be embarrassed if you're not there. They would be embarrassed, however, if everyone found out you ignored them to go on a spiritual journey." She winked. "You won't get in any trouble. We can go in the Silver Dare."

"No need." Erikal squinted. "My new cab is ready enough."

The door slid open, and Meritus sauntered in, glassy-eyed, the acrid odor of the Drink wafting in with him. "Someone said there was a meeting of the council here," he announced, slurring his words. He laughed. "You, they meant. But, honestly, you're missing a great reverie. Berian brought some of the shamans' reserve. He snuck it. Everyone's expecting—" His eyes darted around as if finally taking in the tenor of our moods. "What's going on?"

"We're going back to the maze," Erikal said.

Meritus stumbled back a couple of steps. "Well, alright! When?"

"How about in a few hours?" Cleo said. "In the dark of the early morning, like our first journey."

Meritus poked a finger in the air. "I'll get Alana."

Cleo put her forefinger to her mouth to let him know our leaving was to be secret.

"Maybe I've been called to something," Erikal said under his breath. He turned and rested his hands on his large producer. "Thank you, Giels. Let's be quick, everyone."

The reality of our hasty return to the cave and again committing the worst taboo hit. *Don't thank me yet.*

* * *

The last yellow light of evening clung to the sky while Cleo, Meritus, and I returned to Illyia.

Drummers on a stout stage pounded their instruments. A massive crowd bounced, danced, and shouted, many holding small colored lights that they waved about. The colors gleamed on the metallic hulls of a half-circle of cabs surrounding the dancers. Illyia was already saturated with energy, but this was astounding. I had never seen such a celebration.

Almost everyone wore bright, polychromatic clothes.

"Haven't been to one of these, huh?" Meritus slurred as he patted me on the chest. "They get even more better each one. Let's go. Alana's here . . . somewhere."

Looking down, I rubbed the cloth of my formal tunic.

"Would you like to change?" Cleo asked.

I nodded. She slipped into the dark.

Meritus and I entered the reverie. Maybe a hundred, maybe more, jumped and hopped to the beat. Several boys and girls had faces painted yellow—a seeming perversion of the color's sanctity, yet wild and exciting. My body began moving to the rhythms. Couples kissed passionately around me, and I doubted it was because they planned to marry.

A pretty girl handed me a fancy skin decorated in blue lines and knots—a shaman's ceremonial skin. "Berian's father made it!" she shouted over the noise.

Unlike the conventional, bitter Drink, this one had flavors of grain cakes and syrup. I'd never had anything like it. No wonder the shamans considered it holy.

Passing the skin to a guy bouncing next to me, he likewise handed me a small device emitting several colored lights—red, blue, green. He demonstrated how to slip it over the knuckles to wave the lights around. The invention had no utility. Even the datch game helped hone spear throwing to improve hunting, but this item did nothing but give off light. The colors blurred as I waved them. The Drink had taken effect.

The beats continued to move me. Everyone smiled. I hugged many, each time asking for Alana, but no one had seen her. I tapped another girl on the shoulder to ask, this one in a hood. She spun around, the hood flying off of her head. She appeared to recognize me, but I could not place the blurred face. I blinked to clear my vision and realized that I knew this girl very well. Quickleaf Deo.

My cousin. A shaman. Had no one noticed her?

"Hi, Elder," I stammered, backing away. My vision sharp-ened, and my senses returned. Reality crashed back in. "You haven't seen me." I pushed through the crowd.

"Giels!" she shouted.

Hell, the shamans are watching us. They suspect we might leave.

Cleo stood alone outside of the reverie, peering at the crowd and holding a bundle of clothes. Seeing me, she smiled.

I ran to her with uncoordinated feet, grabbing her hand as I passed.

"Ow. What're you doing?" Cleo complained.

"The shamans are here!"

8

Flight

Leaving Illyia, Cleo and I fumbled south through the dark woods. With the shamans watching us, we had no time.

"Let's get to the Dare Furthur," I said. "We'll grab Alana and Meritus on the way out."

Despite my hazy mind, I'd managed to change my clothes as we scrambled through the woods to Erikal's. The colorful garb wasn't any good for hiding. Thankfully, his parents must have had gone to bed. No artificial lights remained activated in or around the home, which probably meant no shamans had come.

We made our way to the large gates on the balls of our feet as if on a hunt. Anticipating the groaning hinges, I ducked behind a tree. His parents could awaken.

Cleo approached the gates, and they rotated noiselessly.

Thank the Sun. Erikal had oiled them. They closed just as quietly behind us.

Emba and Hola cast their ghostly radiance onto the court and glinted on the enormous metal-clad vehicle. The cab's door sat open like a tazer's extended wing. Pure black shade hid the interior like an ominous portal to the dead. Nothing made a sound, neither in the dark opening nor the forest around.

Cleo grabbed the handholds and lifted herself onto the stepping rail. "Friends? Are you here?"

A chorus of hushing emitted from within. Cleo stepped inside and turned to me. Her body vanished into the black void, but the moonlight still graced her soft cheeks and gentle smile.

Did I wish to urge my friends forwards like they had pushed me to go on our first journey? Was the danger worth getting answers?

Emba, the celestial feminine, nearly round, gazed down upon me. Hola, her younger sister, now just a crescent, followed her in the black robes of Morgoreth. To the east, dark Palis, almost round, sat just above the trees. *Will you give us the light we need?*

Cleo looked me up and down. "The clothes fit you well," she whispered. As I studied her features, the light on her face brightened.

Were the sky gods answering my fears and encouraging me with their glow?

Cleo's angelic smile flattened. Her face continued to brighten, and her eyes, now looking past me, widened as round as Palis.

My head and shoulders spun. Lights ablaze, Elder Sparus's vehicle floated between the open gates, edging into the court.

Its lights suddenly deactivated, and the door flipped open.

Before my head could turn back around, my legs propelled me into the cab's oversized, yawning, black interior. Cleo pulled the door closed with a slam.

Erikal's vehicle immediately rose, dropping me to the floor. The nearby treetops lowered out of view, the entire sky and its thousand stars visible through every window. My body slid back several inches as we propelled forward. Erikal and Meritus stood at the fore, their bodies silhouetted against the heavens.

Grabbing the door's windowsill, I lifted myself. Below, three elders—my father, Elder Sparus, and the young Elder Quickleaf Deo—stood like statues by Elder Sparus's cab, looking up in wonderment, the moonlight and the Sunfire lights of our cab cast on their faces.

Only in the cave had I flown so high.

Our massive wings and all of their facets splayed out like a dragon of legend who threateningly scouted our Deoan settlement below. It seemed the reverie's pounding drums sounded a warning of our presence to the World.

This magnificent vehicle, the delirious camp below, this recorder in my pocket, the voice I now longed to understand, and that we could travel to the Underworld—such a confluence of mysteries had never happened before. It provoked more wonder than any council ostracism could instill terror.

Illyia had been right, its tenor had been right, my friends had been right—something big, something new, touched the world between the earth and sky. And I was determined to find out what it was, gods allowing.

"Dare Furthur!" Erikal shouted. "That's her name." He slammed his fist on the control panel.

My head rattled, and my ears rang from the approving cries. How could the acoustics have so enhanced our voices?

Cleo grabbed my wrist hard. "Who's here?"

Erikal and Meritus drove. Cleo sat next to me. I should have seen the glint of one other pair of eyes—Alana's, if they had found her—but I saw many. Was the Drink still affecting my vision?

"Word got out," Meritus said.

"That quickly?" Cleo asked.

"We're away," Meritus said in a clear voice, as though the

Drink had left him. "No need to hide." Little blue interior lights activated, and several other people glanced around. Alana, still wearing black, sat among them with her chin resting on a fist.

"The Sun, Meritus!" I said. "Couldn't you have talked them out of it?"

"It happened pretty fast," Erikal said. "Anyhow, you didn't give us much of a chance to, what with bringing the elders with you." He turned and smiled.

I grasped a lock of my hair. "Not my fault. Elder Quickleaf saw me at the reverie."

Surrounding Alana sat Fairfox, Berian, Serina, and Samsen— Samsen, the shaman-in-training and elder's son! And a skinny girl. All wore their Illyian clothes.

"Zara," Berian said, pointing to the skinny girl. She raised a hand in a terse wave.

A sharp pain shot from my temples to the back of my neck. "This is a joke."

"Nope," Meritus said. "It's not Berian's Drink, either. It's actually happening."

Word got out, indeed. Meritus had been bragging.

Erikal cleared his throat. "We'll go look at the cave and decide what to do."

"Can't you just drop them off in the commons?" I asked.

The protests were so sudden and loud, the pain in my neck shot back to my head, twofold.

"It's for your own sake," I protested in return.

"Who are you to tell us what's for our own sake?" Serina said. "We've spent months at Illyia. Where were you, Giels Deo?"

Oh, hell, why Serina?

I could have defended myself, said *I've been there*, but to what end?

Instead, I swallowed my frustration and, like everyone else, marvelled at the altitude. We didn't hover or float but flew above the trees. I recognized the North Neighborhood, as it looked like the commons with a sparser canopy. And gardens surrounded square, sunken courts of underground houses, just as Fairfox and I had talked about.

"Is that my home?" Berian said. "Stop. I'll get more Drink."

"Stop?" Fairfox asked. "Is stopping smart? This cab will bring too much attention for your northern-tribe hulkiness to sneak around."

Berian scratched his beard, oddly thick and the color of darkened copper. He rolled his light eyes a fraction. Everything about Berian was light in color and husky—arguably more foreign than Erikal. "Your loss," he said in his rough, low voice.

We glided down a hillside, farther and farther, quickly dropping off cliffs before leveling off again. Cleo rested her head on my shoulder and held my hand. "The moonlight, the sky, it's beautiful," she said. Why had I been so worried about Erikal? She was mine even after failing my storyteller audition.

"Stay by the shoreline," Erikal said to Meritus. "It's wide enough."

The dim celestial light revealed a broad valley. The moons reflected on the rippling surface of a massive body of water, which snaked through gentle embankments and steep gorges. Gasps filled the cab.

"The Great River," Erikal said. We flew high over the river's edge.

Cleo stood. "I'd like a turn." And she and Meritus switched places.

Alana crawled to the space between Meritus and me. *Interesting. Were they together, or did she move because of me?* I hoped she had not. I didn't want any complications.

Alana stared out the window, her face angled towards Meritus.

The Great River opened to the Western Sea, and a din filled the cab.

We turned east into a small river valley: the Camchaw River.

So fast.

The first yellow light of dawn kissed the eastern sky. We followed switchbacks up the high southern embankment. As we crested over the top, the Boromount Plateau came into view, littered with boulders and, of course, the imposing, grazing boromounts.

The rock spires by the ocean cliffs to the west, which housed the Wind Cave, had become a dream made real once again. I quivered. My eyes darted about to take it all in. "Oh, the Sun," I whispered to myself.

"Who are they?" Alana whispered to herself, gazing east, beyond the plateau, where the forest sloped up to a distant ridgeline. From there rose three columns of smoke.

"Who would make so much smoke?" I mused.

Tendrils of hair wound around Alana's profile. Her kiss came to mind. Since then, we had remained friends. But something pulled my eyes to her lips as if taken by a daydream. She did not move. Her features held still. Did she know I stared, and allowed it?

She lifted her hand and moved her hair, wrapping the thicket behind her ear, giving me an unobstructed view.

"No need to worry, Giels," she said. "I see now that you and Cleo are close."

The words, delivered in a flat voice, hit like a punch. Before I thought of how to respond, Alana turned away. She stood and pointed south through the large forward windows. "What's that?"

Everyone searched the direction Alana pointed. Far south, the tree line to the east and the precipice at the plateau's west edge met. The ground sloped down gently there, and the landscape's morphology allowed the rising Sun to grace it with the first sidelong yellow light of dawn. In that bright warmth, several tiny pinpoints of silver moved out from the trees.

"Alana. Your eyesight is truly amazing!" Cleo said.

"People live here?" Berian asked, his eyes wide.

"No," Erikal said.

The Dare Furthur landed near the rock spires straddling the edge of the plateau. At its base, the Wind Cave exhaled Salihandron's fierce, eternal breath. The sound penetrated the cab's shell.

Erikal only needs to push a lever to enter the everlasting.

The objects Alana had spotted grew closer. Several people sat atop reflective metallic pods—a type of tiny, single-person, open-air vehicle about the size of a tassel-goat—that slowly bobbed and weaved in our direction over the rugged land. The machines and their riders' legs smacked through the tall grass and flowers, etching lines in the landscape.

They quickly came within a couple of hundred feet. The riders' tight clothes shimmered in the light, like silver scales. The dark, satin skin of the people created a striking contrast. Only four small wing facets kept each vehicle aloft.

"Southern coast people," Erikal said.

"The Talis!" Meritus said.

The exotic appearance of the Talis didn't surprise me as it did the others. Talis envoys had visited my father a couple of times.

Fairfox stood, braiding her hair into a tail. "Aren't they the Original People?"

"Possibly," I said, "although the lineage is murky." The Talis occupied the land my father believed to have been once called Exure, where the Original People had dwelled.

Cleo opened the door. We, the Five, stepped out while the new adventurers huddled in the vehicle. The presumably friendly strangers, seven in number, approached. Four of them held chromadium spears, whose tips did not end in a point but an impractical, small hole.

"Hello. Greetings. Friends!" Meritus said, presumably to initiate an amicable posture. He bowed low.

A beautiful woman of about thirty, one of the two Talis not holding spears, moved a little forward on her vehicle. She dressed similarly to the others, except she wore polished gold and chromadium neckwear made up of flowing, intertwined, rod-like filaments. She stared at Cleo. "Where you'n from, and make a cab this way?" The woman had a strong accent but talked slowly and deliberately, which helped me make out her words.

"Oh," Cleo said, "you may not recognize us. Our clothes and cab are unconventional for our tribe. We do things a little differently."

Meritus stepped forwards, but the woman did not look at him. "Yeah," he said, "Erikal was able to make his cab this large because of the—"

"We're from the Deo," Erikal interrupted. "The son of the Lead Elder is with us." He pointed to me. Feeling compelled, I bowed.

The woman lifted her right palm into the air. Taking the cue, the Talis collapsed their spears telescopically into stubs and tucked them into loops on their belts.

"Then you'n familiar," the woman said. "I'n Thered, high

priestess of Doren, the Middle-Coast clan Talis. I grasp the Bael tongue. But my companions non't, so only I interpret what you say." The Bael tongue was almost the same as Deoan, because our ancestors had migrated from the Bael tribe. "You happen on a travel and see the cave?"

"Something like that," Meritus said, and laughed.

Cleo kicked his ankle. A smile broke through Thered's austere expression.

"Yes," Cleo said, "we're here to visit the cave."

One of the men behind Thered pointed east and said something to the high priestess in a language flowing with vowels, presumably Talis. They all looked towards the high ridgeline, where faint wisps of smoke still rose.

"Priestess, if I may ask," Alana said in a quiet, deferential tone, "who are they?"

Thered nodded to Alana. "They'n an astray peoples, a poor remnant of confused Underworldess spirits, but they simulate humanity, have life without worldly rules. Here but not here, we name them the mirror people."

"The Lost Tribe," Erikal said to us. He leaned over and murmured to Cleo, but I could hear him. "She seems to like you. Maybe ask about the message."

I had the same thought. We had planned to ask the Talis on our first journey since they were highly spiritual people, but we had not seen them.

"We were wondering, Thered," Cleo said, "if you might help us interpret a message that we think is from the spirit world. We believe it might be Salihandron."

Thered's eyebrows raised, and her head tilted a fraction. "What is the message?"

Cleo turned to me. "Can you show her?"

I shook my head slightly. I didn't want other Deoans to know of the recorder, let alone foreigners. "I have it memorized. It goes: 'Can you hear me? This is what we've been waiting for. From the ether, you have found me. We are of the other world. Return me through the passage.'"

"Ah," the priestess said, "this is what makes you here."

Cleo stared at me. She waited for me to tell them about the other message I knew. But I again subtly shook my head at her. *Let's see if Thered can explain the first one.*

"How did you receive it?" Thered asked.

I stepped forward. "On a secret machine," I whispered.

"Oh!" she said. "Very peculiar. You own this giant vehicle, so let us say I comprehend you own a machine that talks with Salihandron. The purpose will reveal itself with the moons. But join us for our'n sacrament, and as it may, a resolution will arrive now."

The sacred cave sat close enough that its wind blew on us like a constant breeze, but the Talis certainly wouldn't have wanted us to go in. The gods seemed to be throwing up obstacles: first our stowaways, and now this. The reality hit me. Even if we went into the cave, I would return to Illyia being dismantled, to my broken home, and an ordinary life full of disappointment.

What if we crashed again? What if I found no answers about the messages?

My water dragon slid back a little into the murk, leaving a slimy residue of doubt.

Two Talis men laid white, quilted blankets on the tall grass around a tiny flame grill. The grass buckled completely flat under the cloth. The Talis sat, backs straight and hands at their laps. At Cleo's behest, the Deoans all joined.

A high-pitched squeal rose from nowhere. A Talis lady smiled and told us her name, "Doeles," before unwrapping a silvery cloth bundle and revealing a baby.

"We'n here bless this babyess birth with verse, dance, and divine petition," Thered said, "link it'n worldly and otherworldly lives. In the final, the spirits will whisper the childess name."

Meritus glanced at me, rolling his eyes.

Thered stood with her right hand at her left hip. "We will simultaneously appeal for a resolution for you'n message."

Her arm made a full circle over her head, and glittering pinpoints of light streamed out from behind her hand like millions of infinitesimal pixies. An acrid smell rose to my nose, and it became clear that, in fact, tiny fae beings flew about.

To my shock, the mystical beings didn't surprise me, as though some part of me had always known them.

One faerie came near with its sensuous feminine shape. Despite being a pinpoint of light moments before, it came so close that it filled the view of my right eye, though it did not blur in my vision. It wore clothes similar to the Talis's, except hers covered little of her dark faerie skin.

I pointed it out to Cleo, who sat next to me, but she gave me a quizzical look and pointed to her eye. Remembering the pixie was no larger than a speck of dust, and realizing she didn't know why I pointed, I fell over laughing as it seemed the funniest thing that had ever happened. Cleo fell laughing on top of me.

The Talis didn't react to our antics.

Thered held the baby to the sky and faced the Wind Cave. Her voice rose with supernatural grandiosity. "The spirit of this child ascended to the heavens, then looked upon us to choose its mother. The earth gave him form; the Underworld, the breath of life; the sky, a mind. From the womb of his mother and Dayodec the earth-mother, he has come to us. Now we pray." She talked, seemingly magically, like a native of the Deo. Her accent had gone as well.

Following the Talis's lead, we stood and danced around the fire. Thered chanted as we moved. Time ebbed and flowed, at once passing both fast and slow. A jump in my step took an eternity while tens of passes around the fire happened in a single breath.

Despite feeling as though the ceremony had lasted days, when the Sun set, it was sudden and unexpected as though we had only just arrived at the plateau. The yellow glow of the evening vanished, and the god Morgoreth rose, blackening the eastern sky with his starry, velvet cloak. The Talis blankets shimmered in the moonlight of Emba.

Thered's chanting slowly dropped, softer and softer. A gust from the cave smacked us, nearly knocking us all over. And I heard it. A low growl blended with the howling wind.

A single word: "Earthember."

We all fell silent.

The mother, Doeles, talked to the sky. Thered translated: "The breath of the World has spoken. Our child's soul is Saoren. He is my great-great-grandfather returned."

A burst of chatter sprung from our Deoan group. "Isn't it named Earthember?" I asked.

"Silence!" Thered said. "We all hear different names. Only Doeles is blessed with the spirit's true name."

It was for the best. Saoren was clearly a much nicer name for a baby than Earthember, which sounded like something that fell off of a flame grill.

Without warning, the Talis gathered their items, except for the blanket under us. "It has been pleasant for know you," Thered said, her accent returned. "Our'n sacrament is over, and we must return to our'n homes, but keep relaxed. You may possess the blanket and the magic air as a gift."

They mounted their pods.

"Wait!" I said. Thered turned and glared at me as though I'd broken some sanctity. "If— If I may," I continued, "the cave did not talk to us about the message."

She laughed hard. "Oh, non't? Who do you assume you'n? One message means you'n blessed. Is that not enough? A second is epochal!"

Their pods' Sunfire lights weaved away in the dark. Thered's voice lingered like the ring of a bell.

9

The Wind Cave II

"I love the Talis magic!" Fairfox shouted to the night sky. "It's still here."

The Talis had gone. The pixies, just points of light, flew up to the velvet robes of Morgoreth and merged with the stars, glowing no dimmer as they ascended to the heavens.

We still sat on the shimmering blanket. The others continued to chat about the spell that hung in the air. For my part, I searched the heavens for the fae creatures and occasionally caught them moving like celestial wanderers.

Serina played with her fingers close to bulging eyes. "I have power in these fingers, friends."

"Yeah," Berian said. "This magic's better than even shaman's reserve."

Serina pointed a finger at me. A ray of white, foggy light extended from it to me, but I wasn't sure if it was real or imagined.

I glanced at Erikal. "Thered answered our question, didn't she?" If two messages were epochal, as the priestess had claimed, should he and I worry about a few extra adventurers joining us?

Erikal's eyes squinted a fraction. He nodded. "Are you ready?"

"No," I responded. I had too many doubts. I feared crashing, the Guardian, returning home.

Everyone looked at the two of us now.

I stood and walked to the plateau's edge, where it dropped off in a cliff to the Western Sea, and I sucked in the salty air. Emba and Hola glowed above the water. Neither full. My recorder rested in my palm, lifeless. I must have deactivated it at some point. I pushed the button, and the little blue light came to life.

The view suddenly appeared grander than it had moments before—the sea waves below and rock spires beside me—as though it all had been infused with significance. Everything around me allied itself with the enthusiasm that brought us here. The importance of the moment washed through me. *We must go back down. I need to understand.*

My friends had been watching me. I walked to them, my eyes sweeping across our small band.

Erikal tilted his head a fraction and, without a moment's hesitation, said, "It's time for our spiritual journey." He stood and addressed everyone. "But you can only go if you promise to keep its sanctity with us. You cannot even tell other Illyians, except that we went to this plateau." He looked straight at Samsen.

Samsen waved a hand dismissively. "Of course. I'm a shaman-in-training, not a snitch. Prerogative is part of our instruction. Anyhow, you outrank me as of yesterday."

"The rest of you?" Erikal asked. Everyone agreed. "Prepare yourself. It'll be different."

Meritus handed us strips of dried meat as we filed into the

Dare Furthur.

Erikal and Cleo took the controls, folded in the wings' outer extremities to shrink our profile, and pushed the control panel's most prominent lever forward.

We flew through the Wind Cave's black maw. The Sunfire lights cast moving shadows in the twisting, rocky darkness, evocative of swooping demons. The wind howled against the vehicle, vibrating the wings. This time, our vehicle handled it all more comfortably: brighter lights, dampened noise, less shaking.

The new adventurers screamed. Fairfox shouted, "It's the magic!" over and over. I joined in by hollering. But with a calmer presence of mind than on our first journey, my screams came from a sense of camaraderie and excitement, not fear. My life had shifted, taking an orthogonal turn. This time, the descent's intensity did not unsettle my mind, but it shook the murk within me so violently it separated the water from the sediment until everything appeared clear.

The first journey had opened my eyes to my ignorance; this one opened my eyes to me. The first journey induced me with shock, and this one brought clarity. Questions and doubts stopped their rattle. The noise telling me what I should do, be, and think went silent.

No history, no lore, no expectations, no threat of shamans' reprimands skewed the experience.

The last time at the cave, the scenery had overwhelmed me. Now, I saw everything for what it was in that moment: the vehicle, Erikal, Cleo, Alana, Meritus, and the Illyians; the bright clothes; the caverns and the light and shadows dancing and moving among their folds and voids; a final turn out of the rocky cave into another realm; and the innocence melting away behind the newcomers' eyes.

The wind's howling stopped, and the cab's occupants hushed. We again flew inside infinity in the form of an endless metal tube of massive proportions.

"We're moving much faster than last time," Erikal said to Cleo—an obvious observation.

I had been jealous of Erikal. Had I been him—strong, brilliant, and charismatic—everything I wanted might have come easily. I hated the notion and the feeling. But my jealousy of him becoming a shaman had been a gift. It had inspired the argument with my father and my proclamation that I had the magic in me. The statement propelled me to a truth that had played my entire life as the breeze plays upon the leaves. It was a fact I had pushed into the murk, yet was an accompaniment to every song and conversation—every moment.

With the first adventure, I'd been forced to decide whether I would do the rehearsal or join my friends. I thought I had gone to strengthen my relationship with Cleo. But she would have forgiven me for staying home. I had gone not because of something I wanted, but because of what I didn't want: the Equis rehearsal. I hated the constant practicing, speaking in front of crowds, reciting someone else's words like a machine— a recorder. I just hadn't known, admitted rather, that I had not wanted it.

Erikal becoming a shaman and my failure thrust a new decision on me: allow myself to become nothing while he ascended to great importance, or return to the cave and the voice. Was it really a choice? There was nothing for me at home, and Cleo and I finally wanted the same thing again.

Inciting this adventure opened up strength in me, a vista in my mind, like the infinite tunnel I gazed upon. In that clarity, knowing I had magic in me echoed. My own truth hit as sudden and sharp as a lightning bolt in my extremities, and I shot up to my feet.

I've always wanted to be a shaman.

My ability to memorize words did not amount to enjoying stories. From a young age, my parents, especially my mother, had mistaken their desire for my own and seen my skill as passion. The truth had been a creature waiting in the murk, right there before me. I just had not wanted to touch it.

My fingers curled around a handhold and, in moments, we slowed above the continuous platform on the tunnel's lower right. The drivers executed a perfect landing next to the yellow room.

I joined Cleo at the front.

She tilted her head. Her eyes shifted—one moment full of purpose, the next gleaming with delight. "You're focused and unafraid."

"For now." I took in a deep breath and exhaled. It was time for my quiet reverie to pass. My thoughts turned to what waited for me beyond the small room.

We Five exited the cab, the newcomers behind us. Alana strapped a vacuum to her back and waved its wide hose, clearing a path in the dust that still lay on the floor from the last visit.

"The yellow room is real," Fairfox said. "It's so real." She and the other newcomers talked excitedly.

"Shhh!" Alana said.

Alana, Cleo, Erikal, and Meritus advanced through the still-open first door and into the small yellow room.

I stood behind them with the rest in back of me. "This should be your role," Erikal said. My four friends stepped aside. I moved to the second door, beyond which the other world waited.

My hand curled into a fist, and I knocked.

Whoosh.

Dust wafted around. "How did I forget about that part," Cleo said through coughs.

A surge of excitement and fear hit me. Alana's silent vacuum cleared the air, revealing the grated walkway surrounded by a loose confusion of dust-covered machinery, pipes, and supports—mechwork.

The path ended at the stairs that led down. Beyond was a room too big for even the gods, rivaling the breadths of the Midlands in the World above. I shook my head. Except for the open space, everything was mechwork. The distant wall of machines, pipes, and latticework rose to a flat mechwork sky. Mechwork hillocks descended into a mechwork valley.

"The Maze of Azer," I said. Despite expecting the view, it took my breath away. *How did the gods build it?*

Loud chatter broke out among the new adventurers.

"Shhh!" Alana demanded. "Marvel all you might," she whispered, "but the Guardian waits somewhere in this magnificent vista, listening and watching for you."

One by one, we filtered through the door and walked down the path to the top of the stairs.

"At my call, we'll go back," Erikal whispered loudly, "but don't panic or push the person in front of you unless you wish to be fodder."

We stood on the path between the yellow room and the stairs leading down. My hand clasped the path's dusty handrail as if bracing for something.

Waiting, perhaps for another voice, I hardly pulled in a breath. How long would I need to wait? This world had no Sun, no moons, no stars—no time. Yet time passed, only measurable by the increasing hunger pangs in my stomach and the aches in my standing legs.

"Giels?" Erikal said.

"Yes?"

"Do you know anything further?" He looked around, perhaps searching for the cab of the gods.

"Only what I told you, honestly."

"Then this may be our last view of the place," Erikal said.

Maybe the messages had already served their purpose—that I didn't need to accept the world presented to me, that the life I expected for myself was not necessarily the one I should live. And, now, I simply had to determine what to do. "Maybe our journeys have already brought us what we need, Erikal."

But, oh, if only that had been all.

Everyone must have been lost in thought, as no one made a sound. I turned, and all eyes fell on me.

"A little longer," Cleo said.

"We're out of food and water," Meritus said in an uncharacteristically somber tone. "We didn't have time to get enough."

Cleo eyes grew moist with disappointment.

"Let's go home," I said. Cleo's face dropped, and she held still as though collecting her thoughts.

Finally, she gave an accepting nod. And, at the exact same moment, a sound rang out in the air like a single note from a song.

I looked around the immensity. Everyone else did the same, commenting on the noise. It reminded me of a kite's song, but this had an unnatural, dreamlike tenor, unlike the feathered creature.

It could not have been the Guardian. It was too delicate and close, as though it originated directly in front of me.

This must be the sign. Alana must have been right all along. Something—Salihandron?—wanted us, wanted me, here and will protect us.

Walking down the stairs, I hoped to find the source. At the bottom, where the grated path led right and left, the sound suddenly came from my left. Keeping my voice low, I mentioned the change. But others disagreed, claiming it came from directly ahead of them. I followed the music. And, as each descended to the lower path, they too heard the singing on their left.

The song, now several notes long, went on and on. Either through supernatural power or my own curiosity, it lured me along the path into the bright and shadowless caves of mechwork. The others followed. It chose a direction at every intersection in the maze, prompting us through a winding course.

"I recognize this place, Giels," Cleo said after several turns. "This is exactly the route we had taken before."

My memory of the place was not as sharp as Cleo's. I had been too distracted last time.

We continued, and eventually the way opened back into the vast room. "This is where I stood when I looked up at you," she whispered, "and the Wind Cave's shell was gigantic behind you." She pointed up, and I saw the delicately constructed walkway that I had stood upon. It stretched, impossibly, without supports over the mechwork for miles before a hill of pipes and machinery swallowed it on the opposite side. The smooth, cylindrical tube of the Wind Cave lay some distance beyond that path, yet its gigantic circumference loomed like an escarpment.

Erikal, Meritus, and Alana eased past me and out into the open, carelessly disturbing the dust. Alana, still carrying the vacuum device, quietly cleared the air in front of our faces. "Look!" she whispered.

Several pinpoints of light—red, yellow, orange, blue, and white—punctuated the whitish-grey complexity behind where Cleo had stood on our prior visit. I didn't recall the lights being there.

"The cab," Alana and Erikal said in unison. Everyone hushed them.

Alana pointed towards the lights, but only the same, endless confusion of unnatural shapes surrounded them. Nothing far nor close stood out. But what seemed to be disparate parts aggregated themselves in my mind until the massive machine, which matched the color of its surroundings, came into focus. The wingless cab of the gods!

At first, I couldn't discern the ship from the rest of the mechwork confusion, but we stood nearly atop it. Only a gap of about forty feet lay between us and it.

I had only seen it flying far away at high speed, but the machine's shape was unmistakable. The mammoth dimensions, though, greatly exceeded what I'd imagined. It rested on an expansive grated platform about a tree's height below us. From our vantage, we could see just over the vehicle's top.

The cab was at once horribly ugly but beautiful in its strangeness. It was a hulk of an object made up of two horizontal, tapered cylinders on either side of a bulky central hull. The hull, composed of an impenetrable tangle of compact mechwork, contrasted the smooth cylinders.

Those cylinders extended an astounding eighty feet or so. From sizeable octagonal ends, they morphed along their lengths to resolve into narrow, rounded fronts. Ominously, the cab had no windows.

The beast's fangs had spanned the height of the ship, giving frightening scale to the creature. Goosebumps played up and down my body. The world seemed to tilt. I grabbed a vertical pipe to stabilize myself.

Each of us let out a gasp or other quiet exclamation as our eyes pieced together the imposing craft.

The song in the air stopped.

"What now?" Erikal whispered to me.

"Should we say hello?" I wondered aloud. The machine, or whatever was in it, had defended us against one of the most horrid demons of the Underworld.

Despite that, I couldn't help notice that the relatively delicate mechwork above our heads was no more than a few feet thick. The Guardian could tear it asunder. "Let's return to the cave."

Fairfox squeezed by us and into the open. "We should follow this vision where it takes us." She stepped in Cleo's old, dustless footprints.

"She still believes this is a vision," Erikal whispered to me. "From the Talis fae light magic."

"Isn't it?" Samsen said. He was standing right behind me and had overheard.

Fairfox walked farther out into the open to where there was a break in the railing. "A ladder," she said, and descended to the platform the ship was parked on.

"Fairfox," Meritus whisper-called, but she moved quickly towards the vehicle, her light feet and frame barely disturbing the dust on the platform.

"Fairfox," Meritus said, this time louder.

"Shhh!" Alana said.

Fairfox jumped from the platform and onto the ship's side-cylinder, grabbing an inset handhold. She scrambled up a series of them to the top, where she crawled to the vehicle's mechwork center. "There's an opening up here!" she called. "It's ajar, but the clasp is locked!"

"She'll alert the beast," Erikal said. He leaped to the ladder, slid halfway down, and jumped to the grating below, tumbling upon landing. Dust splayed out in his wake.

Cleo let out a gasp. "The Sun. What's he doing?"

Erikal jumped up and raced to the machine, his ripped shirt revealing red abrasions. He flew up the vehicle's inset ladder to Fairfox. They chatted. She nodded and pointed at something. "It's open!" she shouted, and Erikal audibly hushed her. My heart pounded.

Come back. They looked down, seemingly into the machine. *Come back.*

Then came the deep hum. The few small lights on the machine blinked. Did I imagine it, or was the vehicle slowly rising? Panicked, Erikal and Fairfox rushed down its side. It was indeed higher. Erikal needed to drop several feet to the platform and catch Fairfox after.

The entire floor of its central hull separated itself and floated down to just above the grated platform.

No struts or other objects held the descended floor. What looked like dark grey carpeting covered the topside. Rows of something like upside-down angle support brackets, but soft and each about a person's size, sat on the floor. Nothing else, no spirit, ghosts, or creatures, came into view.

Erikal and Fairfox walked along the levitating floor's edge, and Erikal waved for us to join them.

I could not go to the vehicle, nor could I leave my friends. Both options paralyzed me.

Cleo pulled my hand to follow her out, but she let go when I didn't budge. Cinching her dress above the dust, she went to the ladder, grabbing its rungs and stepping down. "I think it's safer there than here."

Meritus followed her. "Agreed."

Their certainty pulled at me to join them. Zara, Serina, and Berian did so, descending the ladder.

Samsen implored us to return to the cave. Everything suddenly felt chaotic. Our group had lost its cohesion.

Alana gazed at the mechwork sky, her searching eyes brimming with worry. "We should go."

A chill ran down my spine. "Down?"

"Anywhere but here."

All sensation left, as though my body had vanished, leaving only my mind. "This can't be happening." I was not expressing dread or disbelief, but a sense of unreality.

Alana's brow furrowed into deep wrinkles. "What do you mean?"

"I'm convinced you were right from the beginning," I said. "We're meant to be here. It's okay if you and Samsen go back to the Dare Furthur."

Samsen immediately ran deep into the tunnel of mechwork from where we had come, turning out of view.

Alana grasped my sleeve, but let go when I walked out into the unprotected open.

My mind seemed liberated from reason. Only energy surged through me.

I grabbed the ladder's rails and took a step.

10

A Search That shall Remain

I considered whether I should step onto the descended floor. Long rows of soft, bracket-shaped objects encased in a leathery material rested on it. The objects looked harmless. Inviting, even, like they might be a nice place to sit. They were called *chairs*, I would later come to learn. In the Deo, we had plenty of places to sit, but no one had dreamt up a chair.

The floor held so many chairs that all of Illyia, over two hundred, could have sat.

Suddenly, just as I lifted my foot to step onto the floor, a baritone voice entered my head. It said a single, nonsense word: "Wenseer."

The sound was loud, crystal clear, and took me by such surprise I tripped over my own calf onto the ship's floor.

"Shit!" I cried. Everyone's heads spun my way. My heart pounded. My entire body shivered from the shock.

Cleo shushed me.

"Keep your voice down," Erikal said.

Although deep and ominous, this voice did not match the one I had heard in my mind on our prior journey.

A moment later, like an echo, I heard the same voice in my ears. "Wenseer." This time, the sound came from overhead, inside the foreign vehicle.

A couple of others cried out.

"The ship's talking," Erikal said.

They heard it too.

The voice again said a word in my head: "Welsai." And again, like an echo, it emanated from the vehicle: "Welsai."

I pushed my palms into my temples. "Is anyone else hearing this in their mind?" *This is too much. Too weird. Stop!*

Cleo looked at me, surprised. "It's coming from the ship, not your mind."

She only heard it from the vehicle. "No, Cleo, I'm hearing it twice."

"Oh, this is craziness," Serina said, throwing up her arms. "Let's go."

"We should try to figure out what it wants," Erikal said.

"Weclensem," the word came in my mind.

"Weclensem," said the vehicle.

"The Sun!" I cried. *Get out of my head!*

Several shushed me.

"This voice is too freaky. To hell with this vision quest," Serina called to everyone.

She, Fairfox, Zara, and Berian rushed towards the ladder. Still standing on the path by the top, Alana gestured for them to hurry.

I joined the panic and ran to the base of the ladder. I tapped a nearby pipe nervously as I waited for the others to ascend. "Faster!"

"Weclommin."

"Weclommin."

"Come back!" Erikal said.

I turned. Meritus, Erikal, and Cleo waved for us to join them at the vehicle. The descended floor now slowly rose with them on it.

Erikal cupped his hands to his mouth. "It's asking us to come in."

Why does he believe that? It must be Erikal's hubris, thinking he knows everything.

"Get out of there," I shouted back at him. "Cleo, come on!"

I grabbed a ladder's rail and took a step up. Above, Alana glanced skyward, and she let out a piercing, terrifying scream.

Far, very far, towards the mechwork sky, two thin lines, slightly oblique to one another, meeting at a thickened center, moved sideways just a fraction. At first, the shape was the size of an eyelash held at arm's length, but it grew larger as I stared.

I blinked and lost sight of it.

"Welcommin."

"Welcommin."

My head spun back to the vehicle. Its floor still rose, and my three friends with it, their faces almost obscured by the ship's side-cylinder.

I moved up the ladder as the others on it gained their stride. I also found the dark, moving speck again. Its size had doubled.

The two lines flapped up and down.

The three on the ship's ascending floor couldn't know the beast dived towards us. A rumble, gentle and rolling, reverberated across the landscape, rattling pipes everywhere.

"Come on!" Cleo pleaded. Apparently, they now knew.

Fairfox twisted her neck to look down. "Did you hear that?"

I waved for her to continue going up. "It's the Guardian. Go."

My friends back at the ship now ducked to see us as the

vehicle's floor continued to rise. "Cleo, Erikal, Meritus—come on!" I shouted to them.

"Welcome."

"Welcome."

Hell, Erikal was right! "It's saying welcome," I hollered. Everyone shouted one panic-driven exclamation or another. I wasn't sure if what I said had broken through, or if they'd heard the word from the ship.

The beast grew closer and seemed like it might easily rip open the mechwork.

The vehicle welcomed us. We needed to get into it. Now.

I repeated several times the only thing I could think to say, "It's saying welcome."

Others now yelled that too.

I jumped off of the ladder, spraining my ankle. I pushed through the pain. "The cab of the gods, now!"

"Move!" Fairfox squealed to those on the ladder below her.

Serina jumped and ran to the vehicle. Berian's oversized body fumbled downward. Fairfox's feet met Berian's shoulders like a rung, and she leaped over me.

I ran limping towards the ship.

Alana! I stopped and turned as Berian stomped past me to the vehicle.

Alana stood at the top of the ladder, gripping the path's handrail, white-knuckled, terror and confusion on her face.

I ran back to the base of the ladder, ignoring the knifing pain in my ankle. "Jump!" I extended my arms.

She looked sideways, indecisively, to where the inadequate covering of pipes, conduit, and metal boxes sheltered the path she stood on.

Her hair fell back, her eyes widened to white disks, and she emitted a scream that jolted me through.

The Guardian had descended close enough for me to see its teeth and the tongue that writhed behind them. And, as if echoing Alana, it emitted its shrill, tormenting wail.

I froze, pain from the sound rushing up and down my body. It pierced my ears as if with metal barbs. I cupped them and cried out, keeling over.

Alana screamed again before crying out my name. "Giels!" She tossed the vacuum aside and hurled herself through the break in the handrail. Her body slammed full-force onto me, throwing me on my back and further twisting my wounded ankle.

I gritted my teeth with the pain, too delirious to think of what to do next.

Alana bounded up, wrapped her arms under my armpits, and dragged me face-up across the dimpled grate, which tore at my clothes and scraped my skin.

My heart pounded so hard I forgot the pain. The devil stopped—its great wings flapped, buffeting my face with wind gusts. Booming thunder shook the grating under me, punishing my scraped skin.

Our surroundings darkened under the beast, who alone cast a shadow.

With its wings outstretched, the sky above filled with the leviathan's bewildering breadth.

Alana dragged me under the ship's side-cylinder, obscuring my view of the creature.

The edge of the rising floor was overhead. Hands from above it reached for Alana, pulling her in. She extended her arm to me as she slipped away.

I jumped up. My ankle, my entire body, screamed with pain.

The floor was at my neck and going higher, with only several feet remaining before it would meet the cab. A few hands grabbed my wrists and dragged me up and over the floor's hard edge. I cried out in agony.

A moment later, with a gentle thud and hiss, the floor engaged with the hull.

"You made it," Alana said, and wrapped her arms around me.

"We're safe," I said. "We're safe."

"What do we do now?" Serina said. After her mouth closed, the "ooooo" in her "do" extended on like a primal scream. Serina closed her mouth and clamped a hand over it. But the sound continued.

The scream came from the beast.

"Hell!" Fairfox cursed and pointed at the large circle of light shining in the center of the ceiling. "The hatch is open."

The cab shook. Dust billowed on the other side of the opening, and a shadow passed.

Another unearthly wail rang out, vibrating the carpeted floor. Pain surged in my every ligament and muscle, curling me into a ball. The world closed in. I started passing out, but another wail shook me to consciousness.

Booms echoed outside, metal pounding against metal.

All went quiet.

The interior dimmed. Monstrous flesh slid across the hatch. It twisted, growing more wrinkled as it moved until it resolved into a black, pupilless eye more expansive than the opening.

"Deactivate the lights!" Meritus said. "Deactivate them!"

Blackness.

The eye shifted away, and dim light returned. Instead of a vast, open space, dust-covered mechwork was clearly visible nearby. The vehicle had apparently moved, though I'd sensed no motion.

A pointed, curved, cylindrical object threaded through the hatch—a talon with the girth and weathering of an ancient tree.

The talon jerked around, its hooked tip scraping the walls. My friends' dark shapes scrambled to get between the rows of chairs as though that would protect them.

I crawled too. As I did, a flat, shiny countertop in the front of the cab molded itself into three-dimensional shapes, like controls, some of which glowed red, blue, green, or yellow.

The massive talon passed by the chair adjacent to me, just as I shimmied into a row. It tore the seat and back, peeling the material away. I screamed, as did my friends. We didn't stop screaming.

Every inch of me regretted our return.

What an idiot!

Gods! Salihandron! Save us!

The glowing controls at the front cast an eerie light, and in it, blood sprayed across the front and splattered on the walls.

The talon pulled the chair by my head, ripping it from the floor. One of the metal legs and its anchor slammed against my neck, flipping me onto my back. The flesh under my chin tore. I tried to scream, but no sound came.

Chairs around me flew, the Guardian casting them asunder.

The great talon left, allowing light in.

Suddenly, a window wrapped the interior where there had been solid walls.

The horrific creature embraced the cab. Flesh wings and bony torso encompassed the view. The rib bones expanded and contracted with its massive breaths.

The cab turned despite the Guardian clawing to keep its hold.

A deep hum vibrated my body.

The beast's enormous flesh wings billowed and spread out. It let go and retreated, but couldn't go far. The devil had taken us into a mechwork chasm.

Two blinding flashes of white light flew forth from the cab's exterior hull and exploded against the demon's emaciated chest—another cry from the beast. I couldn't take any more. I wanted to rip my ears away, but my arms wouldn't move.

White sparks from the explosion streamed and bounced all around, some entering through the hatch. They sizzled upon impact.

Who's controlling the vehicle?

The ship free-fell in the crevasse. But I felt no vertigo.

Enormous booms reverberated as the ship slammed into beams and pipes. The view outside now spun with dizzying speed. Everything inside the hull should have been cast about, but all remained still.

I wanted to brace myself, but my arms and legs refused to respond. The ship rose upward, instantly changing direction. I expected the movement to throw me. Yet nothing had jostled me, neither falling nor flying.

The Guardian's flapping wings, as vast as cirrus clouds, covered the panorama. We followed the creature upwards and out of the chasm.

The hatch shut and clicked into place. The Guardian turned to face the vehicle, opening its mouth of thorns. The entire ship might have fit in its slime-filled maw. Its tongue vibrated as though from a piercing cry.

The only sound came from the wailing of my friends.

The devil turned, violently flapping its wings. As we banked, it disappeared into a crevice in the landscape of tangled ducts and machinery below.

"Alana!" Meritus screamed. "She's not here."

"We pulled her in," Cleo said.

I wanted to stand. I wanted to help search but had no control of my limbs.

The cab shot forward and up at a dizzying speed. Far below, I thought I spotted the grated platform where the vehicle had sat. Nobody remained there. I searched, but the platform receded quickly, and I lost sight of it.

We hurtled into the immense fissure in the mechwork wall opposite the yellow room.

The searing pains in my head, neck, and ankle, which had taken a momentary reprieve, returned.

11

Into the Dark

We were in a place nearly impossible to describe, except the way I had explained the Underworld before—through the window wrapping the interior was an expansive cave, awesome in its size, made up of unnatural things of such complexity that it all looked strangely natural. The whole world was a white, metal-like sieve of machinery, pipes, and latticework.

"How is he?" Erikal said.

"I'll apply more," Cleo said.

Cleo's face appeared before me. She held a metal canister. A grey substance, speckled with black dots, oozed out of it and onto her hand.

I no longer lay within a destroyed row of chairs but rather in the spacious side-aisle. Fairfox, bloodied and with large gashes in her clothes, pushed herself off of the floor to sit up. I looked away from her partially exposed chest. She turned to me, blinked, and looked around as if dazed.

"Oh, the Sun, the Sun, the Sun!" Serina said, standing at the window. "There's more than one. More Guardians. They're hiding under the mechwork."

Cleo rubbed the grey substance onto my neck, and it tingled. It felt good. The searing pain that I hadn't realized had been there dissipated.

I touched my neck. "What's that?"

Pain and relief filled Cleo's eyes. "The voice told us about it."

"The voice?" I said.

"We thought you were dead," Meritus said, now standing over me.

The pain entirely left my body like water squeezed from a sponge. I sat up. On my exposed chest, the black granules from the cream moved about like a horde of infinitesimal ramble-leeches.

My stomach churned and pushed vomit out of me.

All around us, the omnipresent voice of a god talked—the same one we had heard earlier. "Bareselef, elkeai talsa kieltile . . ." it started. It was our language, but a strange dialect, or the words of someone who wasn't fluent. It sounded to me something like these words might sound to you: "My apologeticize. Very scare. No worriesing on yours. Time will be battery and friend gone, but more possible alive—to live. Guardian gone make safer now."

The voice matched the one I'd heard earlier, but it didn't echo in my mind as it had.

"I think he's saying that Alana is alive!" Serina said.

"Who's talking!?" Meritus shouted.

No response. Meritus asked several more times. Still, no response.

"What's wrong with Alana?" I asked.

"She's gone," Serina said.

"What do you mean?"

Serina shook her head. "We don't know. She's just . . . gone."

The others, who all stood around Fairfox and me, looked at us with sorrow-filled eyes.

"You think the god is saying she's fine?" I said.

Erikal extended his hands to Fairfox and me. "Let's hope." He pulled us both up. "Do you know what happened to Samsen?"

"He ran back to the cave," I said. The others gasped with relief.

Leeches, blood, and vomit covered my naked torso. Cleo handed me my torn, bloodied shirt, and I wiped my chest, making the mess worse. "Are the gods protecting us? Where are we? What's going on?"

Cleo placed her hands on my waist. "How are you?"

"Fine, I think."

She turned to Fairfox. "We thought you two were going to die." A tear dropped from her cheek.

Everyone embraced in a group hug. We held each other for a while. Cleo ran her fingers through my hair. Some cried, prompting a tear of my own.

"When does this vision quest end?" Berian said, his voice hoarse. "When do we go home?"

Serina placed her hands on her head; her eyes were distant, glazed. "I don't think we're going home today."

"Why not?" Berian said.

Through the windows, we approached something unexpected. That I saw anything as unexpected may sound a little odd considering all that we had experienced, but its unexpectedness came from it being somewhat normal. It was a feature that could have been at home in the world between the earth and sky. A long, thin, vertical swath of green graced the right side of the cavernous space, and amid that green descended a white, seemingly endless waterfall.

The vehicle passed close enough to see that the green consisted of plant life clinging to the latticework and pipes. Some of the leaves must have been larger than a person, or a home. Huge, colorfully feathered winged creatures, red, blue, black, played in the thin vertical forest. Despite being large, none of the animals had anywhere near the enormity of the Guardian.

"They are like kites back home," I offered, "and we among them." Everyone gazed at the sight, and wonder broke through.

We travelled for a time, and the cavern up ahead dimmed. The bright sieve-like mechwork slowly gave way to dark grey features such as platforms and massive, rounded pillars that dwarfed our ship. At first, the vertical and horizontal structures blended within the mechanical confusion, like shadows among the bright pipes, boxes, and machines. But the farther we went, the more the dark shapes touched and merged into a bewildering, labyrinthine confusion.

It was as though we entered the Wind Cave a second time, but grander, colder, and ghastly with its unnatural chaos, like a forest at night.

"Where are you taking us?" Meritus asked the voice, but still no response came.

Small, distant lights popped in and out of sight as they might in a forest. Shadowy objects obscured the lamps for moments while we flew. But each little glow only illuminated a small area of the grey column it was attached to, as though the darkness consumed the light for subsistence.

As we went, the number of lights increased, but the place grew ever dimmer.

Are they bringing us to Alana?

All my righteous confidence about returning to the Underworld had now vanished completely. What danger had I put us in? Was the ship taking us into a trap? Perhaps it was not real. Perhaps I was right on our last journey, and we had died. We had revisited our homes like so many dead on their journey. I had imagined death as a dream. Could it be so vivid?

"This can't be happening, can it?" Fairfox said, her voice shaking.

The ship moved around corners and bends. Each location seemed endlessly tall or vast, or frighteningly constrained, depending on the moment.

"Dark platforms and shadows, walls, and pipes, everywhere," I said into my recorder while my hand involuntarily vibrated. Talking to the machine soothed me. I did not care if the new adventurers saw my secret device. "We've passed the Guardian. Are we here?" I did not know what I meant by that.

We winded through a chasm within a lattice of structures, machines, and walls. The chasm's abyss extended below and above into black nothingness.

After we turned a gentle corner, the chasm widened. There, among the tangled Underworld, was a dense conglomerate of lights. They dimly lit a vast platform to our right and a cavernous, open space above it, which extended far up to . . . somewhere.

I thought I saw movement among the lights. Yes, things moved—silhouetted, humanoid figures.

We approached. The edge of the platform followed along the side of the chasm. The ship flew just past the ledge, above the solid, grey plane.

Awe enveloped me. Had the messages indeed summoned me to my death? Were my friends actually here, or did echoes of their spirits accompany me?

I couldn't know. Beyond just the physical nature of the

Underworld, none of this made any sense. If I were dead, the Guardian would not have attacked. If I were alive, it would have torn apart my soul and body, or I'd have been cast back to the World, steeped in madness.

"Told you," Berian said, eyes wide, staring at the movement outside. "Bet you wished I'd gotten some skins of the Drink."

The ominous voice again entered the cab's hull. "Friend, we welcome to the Underworld. We like you to be a guest. We help you."

Guest? Have I not died?

"You're Salihandron," Meritus said.

"Ah, a close name. No, Sansar, the Champion. Salihandron?"

Does he use a different name? "The god," I said. "The soul-herder who escorts mortal souls here."

"I familiar gods much. They give ignorance, death, anger."

My exhaustion got the best of me, and I collapsed onto a chair.

"Are you a soul?" Cleo said, and turned to me. "In *The Journey to Salihandron*, the gods subjugated the souls of the deep."

"You understand," the voice said.

The recorder's messages wanted something from us. Did this being? "Was it you? Did you send the messages?"

"We do. You may join us at hunting." Something almost human came through in the deep, omnipotent voice—a sense of cleverness or mischief.

Cleo sat down on the edge of the seat next to me. "What would we hunt for you?" Her voice shook.

"Not just for me. You need no escort. You may come. You may go. So, what else? What god you think we could start with?"

12

Samsen

Go. Go. Go. Go.

Which way? Left—right—left.

Samsen ran down a straight passage, certain he had been there moments before.

The grated floor under his feet vibrated. All around, metal rattled. *What was that! Oh, Sun, help me!*

He searched for a way out of the tunnels of mechwork, hoping to find a reference point to orient himself—any reference.

Why were there no shadows?

To his right, a side-path cut a roofless trench. Samsen ran into it. The enormous cylinder of the Wind Cave came into view above.

Up the stairs, Samsen drew closer to it. He slapped his face, over and over. *Wake up! Why won't you wake up?*

This can't be real. This can't be real. This can't be real.

Up ahead, stairs led to the side of the Wind Cave's shell and the yellow room. Impossibly, he had stumbled upon the way back. He scampered up the steps, keeping his eyes on the grating, refusing to look around at the overwhelming mechwork.

Until *it* happened.

Like a chorus of screaming hell-sirens, the sound ripped into his ears, rending his body and psyche. He fell, knocking his skull on a step.

Samsen begged himself to resist the urge, but his pounding head turned to gaze upon the source.

This is not real.

The behemoth's tail lashed, its thorns scraping and tearing a distant hillock of machinery. It turned to look at him as it clutched the cab of the gods between its bony arms and emaciated torso, then dropped out of sight.

Quick, now. Into the Dare Furthur. Samsen scrambled to the vehicle, stirring dust in his wake. He stared at the complex control panel, uncertain where to start. The vehicle had triple the normal wing cranks. He spun them all to splay the wings. *Disengage the brake lever. Flip switches. Fly!*

He raced through the cave, his arms darting all around the control panel, using his head, his elbows, and a foot when the rest wouldn't do. Why did the damn cab have so many parts?

Under a gleaming, partially cloudy sky, he wound along the Great River. Approximating where to turn, he found the mouth of the Deo's Upper Stream, leading him through strange settlements of gravel-aggregate homes, and up numerous short waterfalls, to the Deo's North Neighborhood.

Erikal's singular vehicle tore through the Deo Commons, the long arrays of wing facets smashing into branches above, attracting looks of surprise and confusion from everyone. Who cared about them? He was home.

Before he realized it, the Lead Elder's house came upon him. Samsen adjusted the wings, but it wasn't enough. He propped his foot up to hit the break-mode lever. His toe almost reached.

Just another inch—

Samsen's body tumbled, rolling over the panel, hitting the glass, then the floor. He landed on the ceiling. The door flung open like a downward ramp.

The Dare Furthur lay jammed upside-down in the Lead Elder's now-collapsed entry passage. Samsen ran to the top of the berm to look down on the home's courtyard, where his father, Elder Moss, and the other councilmembers sat next to a pile of dirt and forest debris.

"Father! Council! It's real!"

His round-bodied father, draped in white cloth, stood. "You're back, thank the Sun. You're bleeding."

The Lead Elder stormed into the court from the home. "What happened to my entry?" His words shot at Samsen like the thunderous wing clap.

He flinched. "Apologies, Lead Elder. I crashed."

The lead shaman emitted a groan that reverberated up the courtyard walls. "Where's Giels?"

Samsen's eyes darted from one shaman to the other. He didn't want to say it. "The beast."

Elensra the Treespeaker raised her wrinkled arm, waving her veiny hand. "Why don't you come down and explain what happened, Samsen," she said in a voice firm but creaky like an old, rusted wing joint. "What is it you're saying is real?"

Samsen wound his way around the court's rim to the back-stair bulkhead, through the house, and into the court. He told them everything, from escaping the Lead Elder at Erikal's to the Talis, the faeries, the Wind Cave, the mechanistic Underworld, and finally, the horrid Guardian taking the others. The whole while, the shamans stared, wide-eyed and still.

"Faeries," Lead Elder Deo said after Samsen finished. He

laughed. "I've wanted to see those my whole life. This is good."

Samsen drifted into a daze. The conversation receded. The council chatted and debated about everything he had told them, but he couldn't take in any of it. Images of the Guardian pounded his inner eye, and visions of the machines—endless machines, pipes, and boxes. What did it mean?

After a time, his father snapped his fingers, drawing Samsen's attention back. "Son—I say well done. I think what we've learned is that my son tells a better story than yours, Lead Elder," Elder Moss said, throwing a meatball into his mouth.

The Lead Elder scowled. "If you can invent a story, it's an unfair advantage, though I'll give credit where it's due. Not terrible."

"Samsen," the Treespeaker said. Samsen's eyes snapped to hers. "We see you are very upset. Everything will be well. You've learned the Talis magic is potent; now you know from experience. This will only help you as a shaman-in-training. Take a seat. Yes. Good. No need to worry. Your friends will be fine. You couldn't have known you were leaving them by the cave."

Elensra pushed the floating platter of meatballs to the young man and continued, "Do you recall whether you left your friends plenty of food? And tents? If not, the Talis will surely find them and help. One of us will even brave a pilgrimage to the Boromount Plateau and return them home if needed." She pointed to the meatballs. "Eat, and let the magic wear off. You'll see everything is, in fact, not at all what you think it is."

Other Voices III

Very far away, a transmission vibrated a moment of time. It trav-elled a vast distance almost instantaneously to reach the mind of the immortal girl, the goddess, as pure thought, as pure consciousness. She heard it as a deep, silvery voice as it passed her and continued through the entirety of the universe.

"Your mind is in the perfect equilibrium," the ancient male voice said.

She touched her necklace. The shapes on the gold pendant moved as her fingers traced across them. She did not yet understand their meaning. "What of the boy?"

"We would not have known the technique would succeed. Your storm did what you intended; he now is in unfettered Entiria."

The goddess let out a cry. It had worked. She concentrated with exhausting intensity so that he would understand. "Then I was lucky! We still don't know if the enemy uses Terminal. And, we are destroying the wrong people, have you noticed?"

"Yes. Balance is waning in the boy's world. That is why you must go and risk it further—to learn if it is Terminal that seeps in."

Will Sansar, the Underworld's denizen, give Giels the answers he seeks and a meaningful fate, or will returning to the land below be Geils's greatest miscalculation?

The epic serial continues with Giels in his very next moments in Episode 3, Dreams Never End

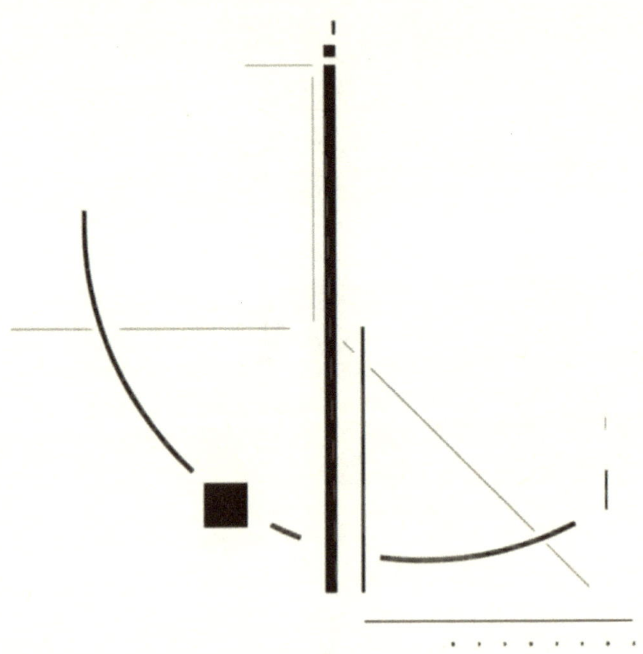